Dead of Night
Nightfall – Book Three

Jeffery Martin Botzenhart

Solstice Publishing - www.solsticepublishing.com

Nightfall – Book Three
Dead of Night

By
Jeffery Martin Botzenhart

To those who have been bullied. I was just like you. You
are not alone.

Part One

Midnight Sun

Chapter One

"And they lived happily ever after," Sebastian read aloud, closing Lydia's story book. Glancing down, he noticed she'd fallen asleep before he'd reached the final page. Holding her ragdoll, Alice, close to her, her expression seemed so peaceful. "Sweet dreams, Lydy," he whispered, pulling her covers up to her chin.

Having sought him out to read her a bedtime story, she'd mentioned that their dad was talking to Abdul and was too busy to read to her tonight. Heading downstairs to get a glass of milk, Sebastian didn't intend to eavesdrop, but nonetheless overheard what sounded like a heated conversation.

"Tonight you were successful—but they are getting closer," Abdul quietly warned.

"I know!" his dad answered, noticeably frustrated.

"This can't go on any longer. A life of hiding is no life at all."

"So I should just walk in to One Legacy Place and shut the whole thing down—just like that."

"No, of course not." After a long pause Abdul tried reasoning, "Lee, listen to me. You've saved millions of lives with what *Nightfall* has revealed. Now is the time you should save the two lives that matter most to you."

"*Every day* I worry about them, keeping them safe," Lee argued back. "But there is more that needs revealed. I just need a few more days."

"What if you don't have a few more days?" Abdul's question went unanswered.

Hearing them drawing closer, Sebastian ducked into the kitchen. Pulling his headphones down over his ears, while pouring his glass of milk, his dad and Abdul walked past the kitchen doorway, both noticing him. Attempting to act distracted, he kept his back to them at first and then turned, acting surprised when seeing them. Smiling at them with his milk mustache, they both grinned back before heading to the front door.

After finishing his milk, Sebastian exited the kitchen, meeting his dad at the foot of the staircase. "Good night, Dad."

"Good night, kiddo," his dad answered, heading back to his study.

Crawling into bed, Sebastian lay there for a few minutes, listening to the song *Edge of the Blade* by the classic rock group Journey. His dad had told him it was his favorite song. As he listened, he recognized certain parallels between the lyrics and his dad's life, being caught up in the power while trying to avoid touching the wrong edge of the blade. When the song ended, he set his headphones on his nightstand and lay his head back on his pillow. For the longest time, he thought about what he'd overheard between his dad and Abdul, the echoes of their conversation keeping him awake well past midnight.

***

"Hey, everyone, *Shakes the half-blind clown* is here," Clay Simms commented, causing those around him to burst out laughing as Sebastian struggled to unlock his school locker. From the corner of his eye he saw them cruelly shaking their hands in teasing. Knowing how they sought to provoke a reaction from him, Sebastian turned his back to them. Increasing the volume of the music playing through his headphones, he drowned out the sounds of their banter while finally fitting the key into his lock.

Collecting books for his morning classes, he then walked away from Clay and his followers, paying no further attention to them, although hurt that Nikki stood by Clay's side. He recalled the first time they met that night on a secluded beach north of San Francisco. He was instantly attracted to her, thinking of her as a beautiful china doll with a tough edge. She had promised to help him but since arriving in Alaska, they'd hardly spoken to one another. This seemed how she wanted it, and Sebastian had accepted the fact she was dating Clay.

Finding his seat next to Scotty for the day's first class, *Advanced Mathematic Theory*, he pulled out his electronic table from his backpack. Accessing the computer uplink to the classroom database, he then waited patiently for their teacher to arrive. In not being allowed to wear his headphones in the classroom, Sebastian was forced to endure the not-so-subtle comments being made about his wearing glasses and his Parkinson's disease by kids in the back of the classroom.

"Pay no attention to them," Scotty mumbled under his breath.

"I'm trying not to," Sebastian answered, looking down at his desk rather than making eye contact.

"That will be enough," Mister Conroy sternly announced, when entering his classroom. Tall and impeccably dressed in a black business suit, their teacher held an imposing stance at the front of the classroom, waiting while a hush gripped his students. New to the school, arriving only days after Sebastian started attending, his strict reputation had spread like wildfire after his first few classes.

In his hands Mister Conroy held slips of paper with test results from the previous day. Sebastian received his grade by text message due to all his work and exams being taken and completed electronically. Experiencing difficulty in holding pencils or ink pens because of the tremors in his writing hand, he was allowed the use of tablets and laptop computers for all his school work. Glancing down at the screen, he saw his A minus grade, having missed only two answers out of fifty.

Addressing his students, his brow wrinkled, Mister Conroy exclaimed, "Greatly expected, with a few exceptions, your test results were dismal. And *please,* note that I'm being kind when saying this. As students in such an advanced class, my expectations for you are high. *However*, we may have to take a step back to review remedial math theories before we can progress. *Of course*, the two students who passed the exam are exempt from todays in class assignment. Scotty Nassir, you may play video games on your smart phone and Sebastian Walsh, you may listen to your classic rock music to your heart's content. As for the rest of you, turn your text books to page *one*—as we *re-experience* our first days together in *Advanced Mathematic Theory*. Bully for us."

Sebastian felt anything but happy at being exempt from the classroom review. Expecting a harsh backlash from the other students, the thought to skip school for the rest of the day crossed his mind. But then he wondered how much worse could it get? Being an outcast from the first moment he stepped into the school, it wasn't as if he'd lose any friends.

Later, when the bell rang, under hateful staring from the other students, Sebastian stood up just as Mister Conroy said, "Mister Walsh, I need to speak to you. Remain seated, please."

Nodding his head to Scotty, he sat back down. Sebastian waited nervously until the last student had left.

Closing the classroom door, Mister Conroy walked over to his smart board, quickly writing out two math problems. Turning around, he then asked, "What are the answers to these problems?"

Reaching into his backpack for his tablet, Mister Conroy stopped him, "Sebastian, we both know you don't need that." Half smiling, he continued, "Just give me the answers."

Nervously adjusting his glasses, Sebastian replied, "34,621 and 21,545."

Tapping a finger against his lips, Mister Conroy quietly asked, "So why did you miss these answers on the exam?" Knowing full well the reason why, Mister Conroy continued, "Sebastian, I fail to understand why someone as brilliant as you would dumb himself down on purpose."

Glancing away in shame, Sebastian's eyes were lured back when Mister Conroy sat down in the seat next to him. "You have a magnificent mind—but you're embarrassed by your level of intelligence. *Why*? Your natural ability in comprehension and complex problem-solving is far more advanced than any of our most gifted students. Your other teachers confirmed this as well, commenting to me that, at times, you chose to sabotage otherwise perfect grades. Why? Please, help me to understand."

Feeling his emotions rising, Sebastian mumbled through the lump in his throat, "I don't want people thinking I'm special or gifted. I just want to be normal."

"There's no shame in being smart."

Unable to hold back, Sebastian blurted out, "I just want to fit in! Since the first day I stepped into this school, the other kids have teased me about being smart and about how my hands shake, my glasses and how sometimes I stumble when I get light-headed." Studying his trembling hands, Sebastian's voice dropped low, "I never thought it would be this hard. I just want to fit in. I just want to be a normal student, nothing special."

"I understand what you're going through."

"Do you?" Sebastian asked, barely able to control his emotions.

Pulling his right pant leg up, Mister Conroy revealed his prosthetic leg, while Sebastian looked on with shock. Knocking on it, Mister Conroy revealed, "Titanium. I've had this particular model since I stopped growing."

"I'm sorry. I didn't know," Sebastian apologized.

"No one, other than you, does. It's not something I talk about, and maybe that's a mistake on my part." Sighing, he continued, "When I was a kid, I lost my leg to cancer. A number of my classmates were less than sympathetic. I'd get one-legged pirate comments from them. At first, I tried brushing off their remarks, but as time went on, they hurt my feelings. My friends seemed to disappear, as I was excluded from hanging out with them. Eventually I learned to deal with being alone. My disability, and being a straight A student, set me apart from others." Rubbing his hand across Sebastian's shoulder, Mister Conroy confessed, "I screwed up today and put you and Scotty in a bad position. I'm sorry. I *do* understand how hard this is for you. I know how cruel and insensitive kids can be. If there's anything I can do make things easier, please don't hesitate to ask."

Wiping the moisture from his eye, Sebastian answered, "Just treat me like the other kids."

Patting him on the back, Mister Conroy smiled kindly to him while responding, "I will. I promise."

***

"I need two volunteers," Mister Orenhiser, the boys swim team coach, called out. Each of the guys standing on the edge of the pool knew what he really meant was, *I'm going to pick whoever I want to. So be prepared.* "Simms, Walsh, step forward." Without looking at Clay, Sebastian could feel his hostile stare. Having been advised by Sidney, his doctor and one of his dad's only remaining friends, that swimming would help loosen the tightness of his muscles and ease his tremors, Sebastian reluctantly joined the swim team. Although not the fastest swimmer, his times were considerably good.

"Alright gentlemen, today we're going to do something different. Since our times across the board need to improve, today's practice will focus on urgency. One swimmer will float face up, down at the opposite end of the pool, and the other will swim out to rescue him. You will have two minutes to pull the floater to safety—or you will be doing some laps for me," the coach instructed.

"I'll be the rescuer!" Clay quickly volunteered.

Exhaling deeply, Sebastian then dove into the pool, swimming over to the far end. Relaxing his body, becoming weightless, his eyes focused on the ceiling while waiting for the sound of the whistle. Fixing his eyes on one of the overhead lights, the brightness reminded him of the sun. Unexpectedly, as if from a dream, the echoes of seagulls sounded in his ears. And when feeling the motions of the water surrounding and splashing over him, his thoughts quickly slipped back to the memory of floating in the body bag months ago in San Francisco Bay.

Gripped with growing fear, his muscles tensed with surging panic. The pounding of his heartbeat muted the calls of the birds, disorienting him with its throbbing. With his head sinking under the surface, his last held breath expelled out in an explosion of bubbles as he drifted deeper and deeper. Consumed by terror, his struggling ceased as he stared out. Growing drowsy, his eyelids fluttered before seeing nothing.

***

Noticing a soft hum from somewhere near him, Sebastian heard voices speaking quietly as he awakened.

"My son nearly downed this past summer when we were on vacation," his dad revealed.

"I'm really sorry. I had no idea," Coach Orenhiser responded.

"It's not something he wanted to talk about. He joined the swim team in hopes of overcoming his fear of water," his dad lied.

"I understand."

"It's my fault, *really*. I should have tipped you off about this. He's just trying to forget it ever happened. Maybe he's trying too hard."

After a moment's pause, the coach offered, "If there's anything else I can do, please let me know."

"Thank you, I will. I'm sure he'll be waking up soon."

"Then I'll leave you two alone. Please tell him I was here."

"I certainly will. Thank you, coach."

Once certain Coach Orenhiser had left, Sebastian opened his eyes, seeing his dad there next to him. "Hey, kiddo, rough day in school?" he commented before grinning.

"What happened?" Sebastian groggily asked.

"You had a panic attack in the swimming pool. The doctor's said you'll be okay."

"My head hurts."

His dad ran his hand through his hair. "They want to keep you here tonight. I'll take you home tomorrow. Get some sleep, kiddo. I love you."

"I love you, too, Dad."

Closing his eyes after his dad left, Sebastian thought back to practice, only remembering swimming out to the far end of the pool and nothing else. As he was falling asleep, the sounds of the ocean and seagulls calling out to each other echoed once more in his ears, causing him to tremble.

Chapter Two

The rapidly swishing wiper blades smeared the hard rain pelting against the windshield. Bursts of lightning briefly illuminated the dead of night, adding further to the diminish visibility ahead. Several times, Lee jerked the steering wheel, driving too close to the road's edge. Flooring the gas pedal, his eyes continuously shifted back and forth from the rearview mirror to the winding road. With his pulse racing and his heart pounding, he found himself unable to respond to Lydia's distressful complaints from the back seat.

"Daddy, we have to go back! I left Alice!" Lydia called out. Cuddling next to Silas, she sobbed uncontrollably while stroking the German shepherd's soft brown fur.

A blaring car horn quickly pulled Lee from his panicked trance, as his SUV drifted over into the oncoming lane. Too frightened to speak, he swerved back into his lane, feeling the car tilt as he headed into a sharp turn. His mug toppled over, spilling hot coffee over his pant leg, though the sting was barely noticeable. Feelings of paranoia gripped him, keeping him from focusing on anything other than the surrounding danger.

His eyes enlarged, seeing high beam headlights now following him. They were speeding closer. Slowing down when entering an intersection, Lee's SUV spun around on the slick surface, jarring his neck. Flooring the gas pedal, he drove toward the headlights. Riding in the center of the road, he waited until the other vehicle reached him before drifting more into their lane, forcing them off the road. Glancing in the rearview mirror, he saw the other vehicle skid off the road, tilting into a ditch.

Racing back toward Sea Bridge, in his mind he mapped out another route to travel in the direction of

Anchorage. But seeing the headlights once more appearing behind him, Lee altered his plan. Stopping at the next intersection, he sped north onto a dark loose stone road lined by dense forest pines. Coming to a stop after driving less than a mile, he turned off the lights and wipers, waiting quietly for signs of the pursuing vehicle.

"Daddy, I want to go home," Lydia said softly.

Still unable to respond to her, Lee glanced out all the windows, hearing the torrential rain beating against the roof, but seeing nothing.

Certain they hadn't been followed, Lee turned on his lights and wipers and slowly drove away. Passing by several structures of a logging company, He soon found another road. Pulling out to the right, the high beams of oncoming headlights blinded him.

***

Over the rumblings of thunder and rain cascading down his window, Sebastian briefly heard an ambulance siren. Occasional bursts of lightning lit the darkness in his hospital room, revealing the time on his wall-mounted clock at just past one in the morning.

The exhaustion he felt from his so-far-sleepless night made him dizzy. It wasn't nightmares keeping him awake, but rather an on-edge sensation. To Sebastian, it seemed like having the intuition that something would happen without knowing what signs to look for. And heightening his stress, his lying there alone in a dark, unfamiliar place did nothing to alleviate his suspicion and fear.

Although his dad had told him the doctor wanted him to spend the night here in the hospital, Sebastian couldn't shake the need to get home sooner. Tugging his cover off, he sat up, seeing a cabinet near his bed. Treading barefoot across the cold floor, he opened the cabinet door, finding his shoes and clothes inside. Once dressed, he turned to leave but was forced to sit on the bed for a moment until light-headedness passed.

Inching open his door, he spied the night desk at the far end of the hallway. The on-call physician, a man, possibly in his late twenties, was flirting with the night nurse. Overhearing them say something about getting coffee, Sebastian felt relieved when they wandered away. Sneaking out into the hallway, he passed by several doors before making his way to the desk. Seeing no one around, he continued on through the emergency exit. Forcing the door open, an alarm blared behind him. Instantly drenched by driving sheets of rain, he pressed his body against a wall just out of sight of the door and held still as voices echoed out from inside the hospital.

"A lightning bolt must have set it off," Sebastian heard a man say. "I'm sure it's nothing."

Glancing out towards the well-lit parking lot, a thought occurred to him to find a payphone and call his dad to come get him. He used them when living in San Francisco, but not knowing where to begin searching for such an old-style phone here would be a problem, like looking for a dinosaur in a space-aged world. Not having a cell phone due to his dad's worries about calls being traced also worked against him.

Being that he was already soaked, Sebastian decided to risk hiking the two miles home through the darkness and the storm. Driving his determination were unsettled thoughts gnawing at him. Yet knowing his dad would be upset that he'd done so wasn't going to change his mind.

Flashing lights startled him when walking half way down the main street. Ducking behind some newspaper boxes, Sebastian stayed hidden until an ambulance sped by. The echoes of a dog barking nearby sounded out, but neither noise seemed to disturb the residents of Sea Bridge enough to turn on their lights and look outside. From one house and building to the next, everything appeared abandoned.

Following the streetlights to the edge of town, Sebastian halted his steps while glancing at the darkness ahead. Strong gusts passing through pine trees branches created an eerie sound, rising and falling with the winds ever-changing velocity. Only the rolling thunder corrupted this humming.

Rain water streaming down the road's incline soon soaked Sebastian's feet, chilling his trembling body. Shielding his eyes with his hand, occasional outbursts of lightning shone the way ahead. With the wind funneling toward him, each step taken spent more and more of his energy, and after what he thought might only have been a quarter mile of walking, Sebastian felt certain that he couldn't make it home. Worse, though, was the growing feeling that something was stalking him, rustling bushes and breaking branches just out of sight.

Further sounds of movement behind him caused Sebastian's quaking body to tense. Nervously exhaling, he shifted his glance back, swallowing hard when seeing the lightning lit shadow of a large bear standing on its hind legs. Turning its head when trying to catch his scent, the bear's bellowing growl struck Sebastian with such fright, that he stumbled, nearly falling to his knees. Yet when the bear moved forward, the rain intensified, masking Sebastian's scent from the beast. Paralyzed to move, he could only watch with dread as it came closer to him.

Struck by lightning, a pine tree just off to the left exploded, sending splintered limbs down to the roadside. Startled, the bear bolted in Sebastian's direction, knocking him to ground before scurrying back into the forest. With the wind forced out of him, Sebastian's chest heaved in an attempt to breathe. Meanwhile, the aches and throbbing radiating from his back, along with the hard rain stinging his face, made him want to cry out in agony, if he only had the strength.

Sebastian knew he needed to move off the road or he'd be run over by the next car to drive by. As best he could, he slowly began rolling to his left, feeling new pains when doing so. Once certain he'd found safety on the roadside, he struggled into a sitting position. A moment later, the rain stopped, like a faucet being shut off. Running his hand down his pant leg, he noticed the fabric on his jeans torn and a searing pain. Without seeing it, he knew that he'd been cut by the bear's claws.

Attempting to brush aside thoughts of how awful he felt, Sebastian unsteadily stood, teetering on quaking legs for a split second, nearly losing his balance. Steadying himself, he turned toward home, with energy borrowed from somewhere unknown, resuming his long trek.

***

Rubbing her tired eyes, Lexia looked up from her computer screen, shocked to see that it was half past two in the morning. Yawning and stretching, she intended to stand up, but stopped when noticing an incoming email. Clicking on the icon, the new message appeared on her screen. Although knowing the source of this email and the damaging *Nightfall* information it would preview for her before public dispersal, her normal feelings of fear were amplified as she read allegations about to be revealed.

Normally expected were profiles of government and public officials linked to the replicate conspiracy, most of whom she knew of. She'd simply scroll down through the list, only mildly interested when skimming through the names. Yet, this email was different. A single profile appeared on screen, that being of General Jaclyn Reddinger. Understanding the general's insistence that *Nightfall* be disable, Lexia held her breath while reading the soon-to-be-made-public accusations meant to tarnish the general's impeccable reputation and spotless service record.

Soon to be exposed, General Reddinger's aggressive assurance to the American public that the replicate crisis would within weeks be contained was, in fact, fraudulent. Implicated in spearheading efforts with the use of replicate soldiers to subdue the break-away states, General Reddinger would be viewed as a liar and an enemy of the state. Public outcry would demand her immediate resignation and derail intense re-unification negotiations with Alaska, Texas, and New England. The probability of a surge in anti-government demonstrations held the potential to rock the fragile relationship between the citizens and the current administration, should it not immediately condemn General Reddinger as a traitor. Thus, anarchy would return to the major cities, possibly sealing America's crumbling fate. Although Lexia felt confident she could shield herself and Dryden Technologies from this conspiracy, the one thing she feared most was the target she'd become in General Reddinger's anticipated thirst for revenge.

Unnerved in knowing this information would be released tomorrow at midnight, Lexia turned away from her laptop computer. Pulling out a glass and a bottle of Vodka from her bottom drawer, with her hands quaking she was barely able to pour herself a drink. And before the rim of her glass could reach her lips, her cell phone rang. Glancing at the screen, she exhaled before answering her caller. "I would have thought that someone like you would hate a disruption with your beauty sleep?"

"My surgically enhanced beauty needs no rest," Sidney replied. Lexia remembered Sidney's transgender transformation and nearly laughed at this remark. Continuing, he remarked, "I've seen some pictures of you recently. You're looking tired. You might want to consider some enhancements of your own."

"It's late—or *early*—depending on your point of view," Lexia responded, refusing to address his comment. "What is it that you want?"

"Just to pass on some news, my dear."

"That being?"

"I'm sorry to inform you, Lexia." Pausing, he then added, "Lee and Lydia are dead."

Swallowing hard, she uttered, "Are you sure? How?"

"A car accident in Alaska."

"I believed they died once before and was wrong. I'm sorry, Sidney. I don't believe you."

"Of course, you don't. The truth is hard to accept when immersed in a world of lies. This time it's true. Have I ever deceived to you before?"

Knowing he hadn't, Lexia ignored the question, instead offering one of her own. "What about Sebastian?"

"He wasn't with them. My source in Alaska is trying to find him. Lexia?"

"Yes."

"You've spent so much time trying to destroy your husband and daughter. What will it take for you to finally admit that you loved them?"

"I'm not going to discuss this with you."

"How can you love someone—and yet hate them so much that you'd want to kill them?"

Barely able to hold back her emotions, Lexia answered, "I wouldn't even know where to begin to answer that."

Following a pause, Sidney unexpectedly asked, "Did you inject Sebastian with a synthetic form of Parkinson's disease? Please don't lie to me. I already know the answer."

"Yes," she softly responded. "Just after I had him abducted."

"Then there's something you need to see. I just emailed you a file. You should read it as soon as possible." Saying nothing else, Sidney ended their phone call.

Picking up her glass, Lexia swallowed her Vodka in one gulp, feeling its burning sensation running down her throat. Then turning back to her computer screen, she opened Sidney's email, clicking on the attachment. Not knowing what to expect, seeing the file he provided proved well beyond what she could have imagined. "*Melinda*," she breathlessly uttered.

Chapter Three

"I made you some pancakes. I know how much you like them," Xavier said, tenderly running his hand through Sebastian's hair. "You should try to eat something."

With his eyes piercingly fixed on the view of the ocean from his bedroom window, Xavier's words barely registered to Sebastian. Over-and-over he replayed in his mind the moment he came home only to find Abdul waiting for him.

"Where have you been? I searched everywhere I could think of after the hospital reported you missing," Abdul said, firmly embracing him.

"Where's my dad? Why were you the one searching for me?" Sebastian confusingly asked.

"Sebastian, there was, last night...." Anxiously turning away, mumbling, "How do I say this?" Glancing back, Abdul forced out, "Something happened last night. Your dad, and Lydia...."

Stumbling back, Sebastian began frantically looking for them. "Dad, Lydy!" he kept repeating, passing from one room after another before reaching the staircase. Then noticing, he asked, "Where's Silas? He always comes running when I get home."

Grabbing him from behind, Abdul held him close, uttering, "They're gone, your dad, Lydia, and Silas." Losing control of his emotions, Abdul wept when bursting out, "There was a car accident, early this morning. I'm so sorry."

Understanding what he was trying to say, Sebastian bellowed out, "No! You're wrong! They're upstairs sleeping!" Unable to pull free from Abdul's hold, he continued yelling, "No!" until collapsing. Soon incapable of even a whisper with the loss of his voice, Sebastian buried his face against Abdul's chest, shuddering and crying uncontrollably.

Jarring him from his memories of this, Sebastian felt Xavier ease down on the floor next to him, resting his back against the bed. This was completely uncharacteristic for him to do. Never one to slouch or even dress down from his usual plaid cardigans, here he was sitting on the floor and wearing a t-shirt and jeans. Xavier then quietly spoke to him. "I know what you're going through." Feeling his trembling hand being taken hold of, he further heard, "When I was a boy, living in Colombia with my family, anti-government bandits stormed our house on night, taking my father prisoner. My father served as a court judge in Bogotá. He had sentenced some of their men to prison for crimes committed. To retaliate, they abducted and tortured him. A month later, government forces found his body." Gripping his hand tighter, Xavier added, "My father was my world, and I was helpless to stop what happened to him. So I understand what it's like for you to lose your dad." Sounding as if near tears, Xavier mumbled, "I lost a daughter, too. I suffer with you over the loss of them all. They were my family, as well."

Sebastian wanted to say something, but the hollowness destroying him inside, cutting him off from all around him, refused to allow him to speak.

Kissing him on his cheek, Xavier whispered, "I'm here. And I know."

***

By early afternoon, with the sunlight almost gone, Sebastian heard his bedroom door open. Taking the spot where Xavier had sat next to him, Scotty held his silence for a few moments before revealing, "Nikki's gone. She left this morning—saying something about going back to Oregon. She left a letter for you. I could read it to you if you want?"

Now understanding what Xavier meant in saying that he'd lost a daughter, too, Sebastian nodded his head while still keeping silent. Hearing Scotty's voice reading aloud, he tried concentrating on Nikki's message to him.

Sebastian,

I wanted to tell you how sorry I am for the way I treated you since you arrived in Alaska. For years, while growing up in Oregon, I was an outcast, bullied and ridiculed because of being different. But after coming here, I found friends. I'm not sure what they saw in me that others didn't. For the first time in my life, I felt accepted and I didn't want that to end.

What we put you through was wrong, and I know how bad it hurt your feelings. At one time, I was a stronger person who could handle the criticism of others, but when I started being one of them, I lost who I used to be. Now, I need to find that person again, the person who had a thing for your soft grey eyes.

I can't imagine what you're going through now. I pray that someday things will be different for you. You will always be in my thoughts.

Nikki

Folding her note, Scotty set it down on the floor between them. "God, she was a pain in the ass," he mumbled, causing Sebastian to briefly smirk. "I wish there was something I could say or do to make all this better."

Pulling his knees up to his chest, Sebastian folded his arms across them and rested his chin over his hands. Remaining silent, he glanced at their reflections shone on the now dark windows, feeling as faded as his image appeared.

Resting his hand on Sebastian's back, Scotty murmured, "I'll come back later to check on you." Standing up, he walked over to the bedroom door, finding his dad just about to come in. Though sounding as if trying to keep their voices hushed, Sebastian heard their conversation.

"How is he?" Abdul asked.

"I don't know. He didn't say a word to dad or me. He just keeps staring out the window," Scotty answered.

"The funeral is set for tomorrow," Abdul confirmed. "I'll talk to him about this."

"Hey, try not to say anything about his foot."

"What about his foot?"

"He keeps stroking the carpet with his toes."

"*Why*"

"Silas usually lay at his feet when Sebastian would be reading a book. He'd stroke his dog's fur with his foot while reading."

Not realizing he was doing this, Sebastian looked down, becoming aware of how his foot was moving and remembering the last time doing this with Silas.

Closing the door, Abdul sat down next to him. Unlike Xavier and Scotty, Abdul remained silent, just sitting there with him. Resting his back against his bed, Sebastian leaned on Abdul. Feeling Scotty's dad wrap his arm around him, Sebastian exhaled while closing his eyes. Willing himself to be strong when all he wanted to do was fall apart. Then, breaking his silence, Abdul whispered, "It's alright. I'm not going anywhere."

***

Stray snowflakes floated through the chilled air, coming to rest briefly upon the caskets before being blown off by occasional gusts of wind. Standing near the final resting place for his dad and sister, Sebastian blankly stared down to the ground. Not wanting to look at the black boxes containing the most important parts of his life, he wondered how he would move on from here. How does anyone say goodbye to their heart? How will the void left in his chest ever stop throbbing?

"Everything is gone," he faintly whispered.

"Not everything," Abdul commented from behind, wrapping his arms around him. Resting his head upon Sebastian's shoulder, he added, "You still have us. Come on, it's time to go home."

Thinking about his words, Sebastian uttered, "I can't go home."

"Not to your house. I want you to come home to mine," Abdul offered.

Deeply exhaling, the warmth of Sebastian's breath fogged before his eyes. "I—I want to stay here—for a few more minutes."

"Alright. We'll be waiting in the car."

Feeling Abdul release his hold, Sebastian shuddered as a cold breeze struck against his back. Sifting through so many thoughts running in his mind, he finally looked at his dad's casket, forcing out words bottled in his throat. "I don't know where you're at now. Maybe Mom's there with you—and maybe Lydy, too. If Silas is there, tell Lydy to take care of him for me." Struggling further with his thoughts, he continued, "Someday—I'll go back to the lighthouse. I know you won't be there waiting for me—but maybe you *will* be there, even if I can't see you."

Stepping then over to Lydia's casket, onto the daisies decorating the top, he gently placed her ragdoll, Alice. "Sweet dreams, Lydy."

Things still didn't feel real to him. Glancing at their caskets, he wanted to look at their faces one last time. But even during calling hours this wasn't possible, having been told by the funeral director that their injuries were too severe for public showing. As for his dog, traces of animal blood had been found in the wreckage, leading investigators to believe that Silas had wandered away, injured, and may have died in the forest. With bears and wolves known to scavenge that part of the forest, little hope was given in finding him.

Wiping tears from his eyes, Sebastian turned away from the caskets. Noticing how the sparsely falling snowflakes had become a flurry, he caught sight of a tall man, wearing a dark trench coat, standing a few feet away. Stepping toward him, Sebastian recognized the man. His teacher, Mister Conroy. Halting at his side, his teacher half-smiled to him and said, "I came to pay my respects to my brother and his daughter—and to you."

***

"Thanks for telling Scotty and his dads to go home for me. They mean a lot to me but I just need a little space," Sebastian said while looking out to the ocean.

"I understand. Do you want anything to eat?" Mister Conroy asked, sitting across from Sebastian in a small ocean-side diner in Sea Bridge.

Shaking his head, Sebastian answered, "No."

With his elbows placed on the table, holding up his arms and folded hands, Mister Conroy rested his chin over his fingers while looking thoughtfully to Sebastian. "You look so much like Lee. You definitely have his eyes." Pausing for a moment, he continued, "I'm sorry that I kept this hidden from you. Your dad was worried about you, especially after finding out from Scotty how badly you were being treated at school. He asked me to come here to help watch over you."

"So, your real name isn't Conroy?"

"No, my real name is Kurt Dryden. I'm your dad's older brother—and your uncle."

"Are you really a teacher?"

"Yes, a mathematics teacher back in Nebraska." Then grinning, Kurt apologized, "I'm sorry. It's just, looking at you, it's as if looking at Lee when we were kids."

"I guess you two were close."

"We were inseparable, even after I went off to college in Omaha. After your dad graduated high school, he got a scholarship to attend college at Stanford. I transferred there so we could finish school and work together, starting Dryden Technologies once he earned his degree. His Daybreak machine was my concept. Your dad made some modifications to my original design and set out to develop it. But I left when business was expanding."

"Why did you leave?"

"Your dad and I had a disagreement we couldn't resolve, causing us to have a falling out. I left San Francisco just before you were born. We hardly ever talked after that. He went on to be a tech billionaire and I became a rural high school math teacher."

"What was your falling out over?"

"A woman we both fell in love with." Pausing for a moment, Kurt continued, "But when your dad called me, begging for my help, I knew I had to come. That's why I'm here."

Studying the checkered-pattern of the tablecloth, Sebastian mumbled, "Thanks."

Easing back in his chair, Kurt suggested, "I want you to come back to Nebraska with me. I understand that we really don't know each other, but I made a promise to your dad that I would take care of you if something happened to him. It's a lot to take in. I know what a struggle this is for you. We can stay here in Alaska as long as you need to. I think, though, that Nebraska would be good for you. I still live in the house where your dad and I grew up. It was a good place to just be a kid."

Overwhelmed and not knowing what to say, Sebastian remained silent while trying to think things through. Reeling from how unsure he felt, he quietly answered, "I want to go home, at least for one more night."

"Okay. Do you want me to stay there with you?"

"No. I just want to be alone tonight. I just want to say goodbye."

Chapter Four

Stepping out onto the deck, Sebastian felt instantly chilled. The grey cloud cover from earlier in the day had disappeared, allowing for the stars and moon to shine brightly. Watching the moon's fluid reflection on the glistening water, Sebastian knew that he would miss this. But it would never be the same, watching without his dad and sister.

Checking the time on his wrist watch, eleven-thirty, he decided it was best to go now. Deciding earlier to leave at midnight, having already finished packing, Sebastian found no reason to stay. Doing so would only amount to the misery of wandering aimlessly from room-to-room with time seemingly suspended. He knew he didn't have the mental strength for such torture.

Quietly leading his dad's sleek, black motorcycle out of the garage, Sebastian was about to climb on when a familiar voice unexpectedly stopped him.

"Where are you going?" Scotty asked, stepping out from the shadowy pathway to his house.

Sebastian responded, "I don't belong here anymore."

"Then come home with me," Scotty urged, moving closer to him.

Shaking his head, Sebastian said, "No. I just...I need to get away from here."

"Then I'm coming with you."

"I can't let you do that. Alaska doesn't have enough geeks. You'll upset the delicate balance if you leave."

Seeming reluctant, Scotty couldn't help but grin when hearing Sebastian's remark. Ever persistent, his expression turned serious when continuing, "I mean it. Let me go with you."

"No."

"*Why*? Why are you doing this? You're safe here."

"The one thing I've never been is *safe*," Sebastian argued back. "Not when I was in foster care, or boy's homes, or even when I was with my dad. I'm like a magnet for bad things. I'm cursed."

"You're not cursed."

"Yes, I am. And I'm not going to let you or anyone else suffer because of me."

"Sebastian—,"

"No. No one else is going to be hurt because of me. I gotta do this. I gotta get as far away as I can." Pausing, he then said, "Tell your dad, thanks for everything."

Sighing in frustration, Scotty asked, "Where will you go?"

Sensing he wouldn't get away without answering, Sebastian replied, "I'm going to go to the lighthouse in Maine. After that, I don't know."

"What about your uncle? Do you think you'll go to Nebraska?"

Sebastian simply shrugged. Climbing onto the motorcycle, he started it, revving the engine once. But then he got off, hugging Scotty, who seemed close to breaking down. With neither finding the courage to say goodbye, Sebastian got back on the motorcycle, making sure to wear his helmet. Waving, he slowly pulled away, leaving Scotty standing there, not knowing if he'd ever see him again.

Reaching the end of the driveway, Sebastian voice accessed the GPS system remotely linked to his helmet. But instead of requesting directions for Maine, he said, "Find San Francisco."

***

Arriving a little before midnight, Kurt Dryden got out of his rented jeep and stood there, looking out towards his brother's darkened house. After watching a cloud partially pass in front of the moon, he stepped onto the metal bridge leading to the deck and front door. Touching the doorknob, he found the door unlocked. Cautiously pushing it in, silence greeted him inside.

Stepping through the doorway, he maneuvered past the furniture, guided by the light of the moon shining in through the floor-to-ceiling windows. Finding his brother's study, he walked in and turned on his desk light. Searching through papers strewn here and there, nothing of real importance caught his eye. "You never *did* learn to clean up your messes, always leaving them for me. And now here I am, cleaning up another."

Sitting down, Kurt opened Lee's laptop computer, touching the power button. It took only one try to guess his brother's password and access all of Lee's electronic files. "Of course, a computer wizard would have an obvious password," he sighed.

Opening several files, he whistled and remarked, "No wonder she was after you." Uninterested in reading further, he turned off the laptop, unplugging and carrying it away with him. Turning off the light, he stepped out into the hallway and headed for the staircase.

Seeing something pass by one of the sliding glass doors, Kurt cautiously approached, holding his breath as the shadows parted to reveal a German shepherd staring back at him. Favoring one paw, it appeared injured. Wanting to let it in, Kurt reached for the door handle, but the dog backed away. A moment later, it hobbled out of sight. Kurt opened the door, thinking to follow, but once outside, he couldn't find it anywhere. After a few minutes, he returned to the house.

On the second floor, he glanced in through the open doors of two bedrooms and a bathroom before approaching a closed door. Believing this was Sebastian's room, he pressed down on the door handle and slightly pushed the door in. Spying inside, he saw the unmade bed and stepped in to find Sebastian missing.

Returning to the hallway, Kurt leaned against the wall, closing his eyes and running his hand through his hair before pulling out his cell phone. He pressed his home number, waiting for a minute before a woman's voice answered.

"Hello."

"It's me. I'm sorry to wake you," Kurt apologized.

"It's alright. I miss you."

"I miss you, too." Exhaling, Kurt asked, "Did they arrive?"

"Yes, this evening. It feels strange having them here."

"I understand," Kurt responded. "Have you changed your mind about this?"

"No. You said it's what Lee wanted if something happened."

"I wouldn't blame you for not wanting to go through with this."

Changing the subject, she asked, "When are you coming home?"

"My flight from Anchorage to Seattle leaves at eight in the morning. My connecting flight to Omaha leaves at noon. I should be home tomorrow evening sometime."

"Is Sebastian coming with you?" she asked.

"No, he's gone."

"Gone? *Where*?" she blurted out.

"I don't know. Maybe it's for the best." After a long pause, Kurt asked, "Are you still there? Melinda?"

"Yes, I'm still here. I love you."

"I love you, too. I'll be home as soon as I can."

***

"Just one little pill swallowed every day. That's all it takes," Lexia whispered while staring at a small yellow tablet pinched between her index finger and thumb. Called *'the happy pill'* by some, Ceravoraxinal was the latest experimental drug she'd been prescribed for treating her bipolar disorder. The side effects included severe nausea, suicidal tendencies, and brain aneurism in some patients. For Lexia, it meant debilitating migraine headaches, vomiting, muscle spasms, and the occasional nose bleed.

Diagnosed bipolar in her teens, Lexia's parents made certain that no one would find out. Fearing her exclusion from Somalia's Olympic track team, her disorder was kept secret in the highest levels of the country's sports officials as it was hoped she would earn a gold medal for Somalia. Labeled as *difficult* and *a menace* among other athletes, while prone to what some considered legendary mood swing bordering on violence, she was shunned by most of her competitors. When finally reaching the pinnacle of her distance running career, her disqualification in a preliminary heat at the 2012 London Olympic Games tarnished her previous achievements. Branded a national disgrace by her countrymen, she vowed never to return to Somalia.

Sipping some wine, Lexia remembered meeting Lee in London and how their brief introduction led to a tumultuous love affair. Even from Lee, she kept her bipolar disorder hidden. And after a few years of depression and extreme mood swings, she'd driven him into Melinda's arms. Eventually he found his way back to her after Melinda's death and his son's abduction, both planned by her. Lexia knew Lee no longer loved her and was always perplexed by why he returned to her, but in the end, when unleashing *Nightfall*, Lee's motive became clear. Revenge.

She'd been so careful to cover her tracks and eliminate loose ends which could lead investigators to her. However, her deep love for him somehow blinded her in missing the most minor detail. Remembering something

Sidney said to her, *"How can you love someone and yet hate them so much that you'd want to kill them?"*

Lexia knew the answer to this. When suffering through a bipolar episode, such extreme hatred filled her. And in the midst of this, urges to kill and destroy were insatiable. It was like opening Pandora's Box and standing back, watching the evil and ensuing devastation.

"I've killed my husband—and my daughter—and have nearly killed my son," she uttered, her eyes crazed on the threshold of hysterics. The detailed explanation of Melinda's infertility was revealed in the information sent to her by Sidney. Unable to conceive a child, at Lee's request, Sidney stole one of Lexia's harvested eggs, implanting it inside Melinda. And through genetic alterations, the embryo was designed to be a male. When Joshua, or rather Sebastian, was born, Lexia held the distinction of being his biological mother, while Melinda was merely a surrogate. Thinking of Sebastian, Lexia choked out, "I injected him with a disease and I nearly blew his brains out with a gun. What kind of monster am I?"

Moving to pour herself another glass of wine, Lexia's attention was drawn to her television. Appearing on screen, General Jaclyn Reddinger's image sent a chill down her spine. Turning up the volume, she heard the news announcer say, "We interrupt this broadcast from breaking new in Washington, DC. Through revelations just released from the latest *Nightfall* data breach, staggering allegations implicating General Jaclyn Reddinger in a replicate military scandal are rocking the American government to its core. Sources close to the President say that he had no knowledge of the general's plans to use sophisticated military replicates in planned invasions of the breakaway states of Alaska, Texas, and six New England states. Both New England and Alaska are said to be considering withdrawing their negotiators, with no word yet from Texas regarding the status of their delegation.

Efforts to directly contact General Reddinger over these allegations have failed. A spokesman at the Pentagon remained silent when asked about the general's current location. As information is gathered over this breaking story, we will keep you updated. Now back to our regularly scheduled program."

Flinging the yellow capsule aside, Lexia raised the wine bottle to her lips but stopped drinking when her television screen flickered. The late-night show she'd been watching suddenly disappeared, replaced with the appearance of her bedroom. Rising slowly from her bed, Lexia's jaw dropped when watching her onscreen image mimic her every movement. Stepping over to a wall of sliding glass doors, she looked outside. Paralyzed to move further, Lexia's eyes locked on the silhouette of a drone hovering in front of the lustrous moon. Obviously equipped with a spy cam, the fear coursing through her intensified when blinded by a red laser beam. Dropping to the floor, each door shattered in unison, spraying shards of glass in every direction. The far interior wall was also riddled with bullets, several hitting the television, causing it to explode with fire and sparks.

With her ears ringing from the blast of gunfire, Lexia barely heard the buzzing of her cell phone. Crawling over to it, when looking down at the screen, she read the message, *I'm coming for you.*

Chapter Five

"I like this tire swing," Lydia called out, her long hair flowing in the breeze.

"I'm glad you do, Princess," Lee answered, continuing to push the tire to make her go higher. Gazing off in the wide-open distance, he could see the pale orange sun hanging low on the western Nebraska horizon. A more vibrant shade of orange blended in with hues of blue in the multi-colored sky. Smiling while listening to her joyful laughter, the peacefulness of his thoughts challenged the notion that one could never go home.

Glancing to his right, Lee saw the large red barn, a favorite place to play hide and seek with Kurt when they were boys. The smell of hay from the loft reminded him of fortresses they built and battles to conquer each other's. And he remembered his morning chores, caring for the farm animals before riding the bus to school. A few times, he had to chase the bus when being too slow in finishing milking the cow or collecting eggs from the hens.

To his left, he looked at their large white farmhouse with its wrap-around porch. Memories of his parents sitting there on summer nights, listening to the radio while watching him and Kurt catch lightning bugs, revisited his thoughts. Each memory of this place seemed as if happening just yesterday. How had so many years gone by?

"When is Sebastian coming?" Lydia asked. "I miss him."

Not sure how to answer her question, Lee finally said, "I don't know. I miss him, too." Feeling guilty in leaving Sebastian behind, Lee silently cursed himself. But he knew there was no way Sebastian could follow them here. Certain he'd never see his son again, his heart sank deep in his chest, leaving him hollow inside.

Breaking him from his thoughts, Lydia said, "Let's go for a walk."

"Alright, Princess," he responded, slowing down her swing until it came to a stop. Grabbing his hand, Lydia pulled him along through the front yard out to the dirt road. "Which direction do you want to go?"

"This way," Lydia replied, dragging him to the right. Releasing his hand, she skipped ahead, bending down every so often to collect wild flowers growing in the tall swaying grass. Lydia then stopped, distracted by the overhead flight of a crow. Another, perched on a post across the road, cawed at her. Holding her white dress, she politely curtsied to it before it took off. Waving to it, Lydia continued on, expressing wonder with her surroundings simply with her smile. Watching her closely, Lee understood that having her with him was a blessing he never imagined, his saving grace.

Arriving at an intersection half mile down the road, Lydia stopped skipping. Appearing confused, she turned back to Lee, asking, "Which way do we go now?"

"Back to the house," Lee answered.

"But where do these roads lead?"

Pointing ahead, Lee responded, "Well, going straight ahead, we would eventually reach Wyoming. By walking south we'd go to Kansas and if walking north we'd be in South Dakota."

"Let's keep walking straight," she said.

"We can't. This is the end of the program in this direction," Lee revealed.

"*Program*? What does that mean?" Lydia confusingly wondered.

***

After a week's ride, stopping many times when his tremors and light-headedness forced him to pull off the road, Sebastian reached San Francisco just after sunrise.

Listening to music sounding through his motorcycle helmet, another of his dad's favorite classic rock songs, *Troubled Child*, reminded him of what he faced in returning to San Francisco. Like the youth in the song, he too was miles away from trusting anyone but determined to find enough faith to survive on his own.

Before venturing further into the city, he drove to a warehouse district, arriving at a place he'd heard rumors of. Pulling up to what looked like an abandoned building, Sebastian parked the motorcycle, then banged on a metal door. A minute later, a young, blonde-haired woman decorated with colorful tattoos covering her exposed arms, appeared in the doorway.

"Yeah, sugar, you knocked?

"Are you Vixen?"

"Depends on who's asking?" she replied. "You're a little young for my taste."

"I'm not here selling myself," Sebastian responded. Motioning toward the motorcycle, he asked, "How much would you give me for it?"

Strolling around it, Vixen kicked the tires and glided her fingers across the sleek black frame. "Is it stolen?"

"Borrowed," Sebastian answered, causing her to smile.

"You've got expensive taste," she commented as she walked over to him. Playfully running her hand through his hair, she offered, "I'll give you a thousand for it."

"Done," Sebastian agreed.

Laughing, she remarked, "You might want to improve your bargaining skills, sugar. I would have paid three thousand." Vixen left him alone, walking back into the building.

Gathering his possessions from the motorcycle, not once did he think about keeping it. Wanting to forget as much as he could, Sebastian made certain to keep few things that would remind him of his dad.

Returning from inside, Vixen hand him one thousand dollars and softly kissed his cheek.

Crookedly grinning, Sebastian revealed, "You know, I would have taken five hundred. Maybe *you* should improve *your* bargaining skills." Crossing her arms, clearly surprised by his remark, Sebastian felt her stare as he walked away.

***

An hour later, as the sun was setting through a multi-colored sky of blue and orange, Sebastian climbed up the fire escape to the abandoned utility room he once called home. Opening the metal door, he gazed in, seeing everything untouched from when he was last here. The books he'd rescued from dump site lined his shelves, each waiting to be read again. His unmade cot appeared less than inviting with the copy of *The Catcher in the Rye* resting on his pillow, and strewn about were his salvaged clothes and basketball.

Instead of going inside, Sebastian walked over to the roof's edge. Looking out, the impressive, towering skyline of San Francisco had begun its glittering in the fading light. Trams glided along their suspended rails, carrying the city elite. He remembered nights just sitting and watching, wondering what life away from San Francisco could be like. But now, having memories of times gone from the city, he was filled with regret of ever having left. Sensing how his emotions might overwhelm him, Sebastian swallowed hard and thought to himself, *how do I forget everything that happened? How do I find my way back to my life from before?*

Leaning against a brick wall, he closed his eyes. A rush of faces soon intruded his thoughts, his dad and sister, Scotty and his dads, and even Harry. Sebastian repeatedly mumbled, "Go away. Go away," while pounding his fist against his head. Then slouching down, his pulse racing and his chest throbbing and heaving, Sebastian sobbed. No matter how much he wanted to forget everything, he knew he'd never be able to.

**

Sitting out on the porch swing, listening to the sounds of the Nebraska night, Melinda pulled her shawl tighter around her. Not wanting to be inside because of Lee and Lydia now being here, the outside had become her refuge. But even outside, she found no peace from torturous thoughts.

Thinking back years ago to that afternoon before the car accident, terrible memories of her phone conversation with Lexia remained vivid in her mind.

"Everything has been taken care of. All you need to do is to pretend that your son is sick and in need of seeing a physician. Kurt will be waiting at the hospital for you and your son. I'll provide a distraction while the three of you sneak away," Lexia said. *"Melinda, are you there?"*

"Yes," she answered anxiously.

"By working together, both of us will have everything we want," Lexia offered. *"You and your son can be with Kurt, the man you've always loved. And I'll get Lee and Lydia back. Knowing how Lee and his brother are estranged, you should never need worry that Lee will find out."*

"Are you sure this will work?"

"Trust me," Lexia calmly answered. *"No one will see this coming."*

True to Lexia's words, no one saw what was coming. Lee had been taken to a different hospital and told that she had died. Awakening in a hospital after the accident, she remembered seeing Kurt and him telling her that Joshua was swept away by the river current, as told to him by Lexia. The devastation she felt over the tragic death of her son left her reeling with guilt for years. After recovering from her injuries, Kurt brought her to Nebraska where they assumed a quiet life, and although she loved Kurt, the void in not having her son with her left a specter to haunt her, spoiling the life she imagined and hoped for.

Melinda then remembered how elated she felt when learning of Lee contacting Kurt after so many years, revealing to him that Joshua was alive, using the name, Sebastian. With Lee's begging for Kurt's help in protecting Sebastian, the thought of having her son back changed from a sweet dream to a reality. One thing, though, held her back from being with Sebastian. Lexia's deadly threat, that if Melinda ever revealed to Lee she was still alive, could cost both her and Kurt's life. Fearful that Lexia would not only harm Kurt, but also Sebastian, forced her to remain hidden. The unexpected turn of events, bringing Lee and Lydia here, however, changed everything. All Kurt had to do was bring her son back to Nebraska with him. But finding out that Sebastian had run away felt like a knife slashing through what remained of her heart.

Startled when seeing headlights approaching, Melinda stood up, holding her breath in waiting to see who was coming. Exhaling with relief when recognizing Kurt's pickup truck, she stepped off the porch and eagerly waited for him. Kurt's smile and wave restored her courage, which was beginning to falter.

"Hey, beautiful," he greeted her, dropping his suitcase as she rushed into his arms. Kissing him several times, she held his hand while taking a step back. "I'm sorry I was gone so long."

"I understand why," she responded, trying to smile. Turning away, she felt Kurt's arms wrap around her. "How was he? Before he left?" she finally struggled to ask.

Whispering to her, Kurt answered, "I'm not going to lie to you. Sebastian went through hell. He's lost and damaged and fragile. And he's sick."

Shocked by this, Melinda shifted back. "What do you mean?"

Pausing, Kurt revealed, "Sebastian has Parkinson's disease. He takes medicine to control it, but he'll never be cured."

"What have I done?" Melinda mumbled.

"You didn't cause this," Kurt corrected her.

"Yes, I did. It's all my fault," she insisted. "I know I sold my soul to a demon so that we could have a life together as a family."

Pushing strands of her fallen hair aside, Kurt responded, "No, *we* sold *our* souls to the devil, not understanding what she could be capable of." Further reasoning, Kurt said, "If my brother had found out about us, he never would have allowed you to have any sort of custody of your son. I know how desperate you were and why you asked for Lexia's help. We just underestimated how evil she could be."

Tearfully, Melinda muttered, "We need to find him before she does."

Kissing her moist cheek, Kurt whispered, "I know."

Chapter Six

Having fallen asleep outside, a noise from the alley down below startled Sebastian awake. Peering over the roof's ledge, he spied a boy rummaging through one of the dumpsters. Through the dim light below, he instantly recognized the boy's grey shirt, knowing he was from the San Gabriel Boys Shelter. While watching him, he saw the boy slip, his leg getting wedged between the dumpster and the building.

Climbing down the fire escape, Sebastian cautiously approached the boy, starling him when he said, "You look like you could use some help." With his eyes enlarged by fear, the boy stayed silent, quaking while watching Sebastian approach. "You know, this would go easier if you told me your name."

"Liam," he mumbled.

"I'm Sebastian."

Walking up to him, Sebastian noticed Liam's bald head under his baseball cap and how pale and emaciated his skin and body appeared. Seeming to understand why Sebastian was looking so closely at him, Liam offered, "I know I look different from others. I'm allergic to the sun. My skin burns and blisters if I'm even exposed to sunlight for just a minute. The other boys at San Gabriel think I'm a vampire."

"I'm sorry, Liam. I know how mean the boys at San Gabriel can be."

"You were there?"

"Yeah, it's a bad place," Sebastian commented while trying to free him. "How old are you?"

"I'm twelve, although I only look about eight or nine."

Huffing and pushing hard, he was able to shift the dumpster enough to free his leg. Feeling a little light-headed, Sebastian sat down on a crate.

"Are you okay?"

"Yeah, I'm just a little tired." Looking at Liam, Sebastian asked, "How long have you been at San Gabriel? I escaped from there in June. I don't remember you."

"I was brought there by social services at the end of July. I was living at a shelter in Oakland, but because of overcrowding I was transferred to San Gabriel."

Chuckling, Sebastian commented, "I bet they didn't know how overcrowded San Gabriel is, or how terrible the people are who run it."

With a large shadow appearing from behind him, Sebastian watched Liam's expression explode with fear before he bolted away, knocking a trash can over as he ran down the alley. Crying out in pain, a large black hand's crushing grip on his neck sent Sebastian kneeling down. And then before his eyes appeared a familiar man.

"Why *Sebastian*, how wonderful to finally find you."

Staring up, he saw the smirking face of Darrin Bender, the head administrator of the San Gabriel Boys Shelter. Without looking back, he knew that Bender's henchman, LeShun Blake, was the man holding him. When dragged to his feet, LeShun's chokehold left Sebastian gasping for air.

Into his ear, LeShun rasped, "The other boys will so enjoy seeing you again."

"Mister Blake, I believe we should be getting back to the shelter," Bender calmly commented. "Sebastian, here, needs his rest after such an ordeal of being away. And I believe his re-indoctrination with our rules and regulations should commence as soon as possible. I'm certain we do not wish for his questionable exploits these past months to taint the impressionable thoughts of his brothers at San Gabriel."

With the air flow to his lungs almost cut off by LeShun's hold, Sebastian felt light-headed a moment before passing out.

***

Jolted awake from unconsciousness, near-freezing water pummeled Sebastian against a cinder-block wall. Stripped of his shirt, the forceful spray from the hose stung and bruised his exposed skin. Having lived through this cleansing ritual before, Sebastian remembered not to shield his body or suffer the consequences of re-cleansing. Pointed at his face, he could barely breathe until the gushing water abruptly stopped. Buckets of disinfectant soap where then poured over him, leaving him thankful that he couldn't smell the heavy stench of lye. Coughing and vomiting out some of the disinfectant that seeped into his mouth, no moment's rest was found as the hose once more doused him with its harsh stream of water.

With the outer cleansing now complete, the inner cleansing started, designed to purge one's body of what Bender described as '*toxins.*' Anything not stale, mold-encrusted, or rotting was considered to be harmful to the body. With his head forced back and his jaw pried open, a bottle of castor oil was placed to his lips. By drinking the full bottle and then vomiting, a body would be deemed clean inside. Again, understanding the ritual, Sebastian willingly swallowed every gulp. Moments later, he threw up into a metal bucket.

Dragged away to a dimly lit room, the re-indoctrination of house rules, based on the theory of perpetual penance, commenced for Sebastian when reunited with the boy elders, Lucas and Jaxson, both seventeen-years-old. Strong, well nourished, and trained in self-defense tactics, their re-introduction began with slapping his face until bloodied. Then dipping their fingertips in his streaming blood, they spelled righteous words across his chest and torso before beating these words into his skin by vigorous jabs from their fists.

Hearing someone enter the room, Sebastian saw Bender through his swollen eyes, thoughtfully looking into his face. "Well done, gentlemen. Now, I believe our friend, Sebastian, has reached the point of absolution from his peers. Please lead him on his pilgrimage through his gathered brothers before his arrival in the reflection chamber." Addressing him directly, Bender whispered, "Sebastian, as a reminder, when entering the chamber I would caution your reflection to be silent. When one cries out in pain, it shows an internal struggle with the devil forcing the elders to reiterate the house rules using more conviction with their teaching."

Nodding his head to Lucas and Jaxson, each stood opposite the other, pulling Sebastian to his feet. Holding him up, after passing through doors that were locked behind them, Sebastian opened his eyes to many boys lining both sides of a path to a door at the far end of a gymnasium-sized room. With high windows and rows of bunks, three beds high, well over one hundred boys called this home or hell, depending upon the boy's level of courage or insanity.

Releasing Sebastian to walk or crawl on his own, he took two steps before stopping in front of the first few boys. From his quivering, swollen lips, he uttered, "Forgive me, brothers, for I have sinned." Each boy then proceeded to spit upon him, offered celebratory remarks by the elders if the saliva landed on Sebastian's face. Staggering ahead a few steps, Sebastian echoed his words, "Forgive me, brothers, for I have sinned."

Halfway across the room, his legs gave out, forcing him to crawl. When moving too slowly, he felt one of the elders tap against his bare foot, silently prompting him to quicken his pace. Again, understanding the ritual, should he stop or collapse, they would drag his body back and force him to begin again. Even worse, saliva would be replaced by urine. Failing to understand how he found the strength to continue on, Sebastian crawled and then stood again when nearly finished.

Drenched with spit once he'd reached the far end of the room, Lucas opened the door, kicking Sebastian inside and locking the door behind him. Falling forward, he landed atop the cold concrete floor. Keeping his breathing shallow while stifling any groaning from his agonizing pain, Sebastian kept his eyes closed, hoping to pass out.

***

Sometime later, Sebastian felt his body being rolled over. Unable to open his eyes due to the swelling, he felt a cool, wet sensation lightly gliding across his throbbing face. "You took it real bad," a soft voice faintly whispered.

"Who?" Sebastian choked out.

"Shhh, I'm Liam. You saved me in the alley. Don't speak. I'm gonna take care of you." After a long pause, Liam added, "Thank you."

Thinking that Liam had escaped from Bender, Sebastian now wondered how they'd caught him. He also wondered why Liam didn't seem as in bad shape as he was. Somehow, Liam must have read his mind.

"About a month ago, I found a way to sneak in and out of here. I only leave during the night and come back just before sunrise. I hide in the air ducts. Bender keeps trying to catch me but I keep getting away. It's pretty easy for me to slip in and out through tight spaces because I'm pretty scrawny. A guy like you, with muscles, won't be able to get out the way I do."

Remembering his previous escape from this place, Sebastian thought about how unexpected and easy it had been. *Having been locked here in the reflection chamber for refusing to punish a younger boy for eating a second piece of bread at dinner, when an early morning earthquake forced an evacuation, he'd been left behind. No one thought to get him. The initial quake damaged the lock, causing the door to swing open. Sebastian simply walked out to an empty building. When wandering through the halls he'd never been allowed down before, he found an exit door and stepped outside. With no one around, he just kept walking. Taking off his San Gabriel shirt, he stole a skateboard from a nearby park, riding it down the street. Being that it was early June and warm, no one seemed to pay attention to a shirtless teen skater.*

While continuing to tend to Sebastian's cuts, Liam guessed an obvious unspoken question. "So why don't I just run away? Where would I go? I'm scared out there. And what would people think when they saw me? Somebody would call the cops and then I'd be brought back here." Sounding ashamed, Liam added, "I'm sorry you got caught tonight. Like I said, they've been trying to catch me for a couple of weeks now. If they ever do, they won't bother with re-indoctrination. I'm pretty sure they'll kill me."

"Sorry," Sebastian breathlessly uttered.

"Shhh, it's okay." The sound of a package opening was followed by something touching his mouth. "Eat this. It's chocolate. You'll need your strength."

"Thanks."

"Shhh! Gosh, you talk a lot," Liam commented. Sebastian tried smiling, but his face hurt. Noticing movement near his ear, Sebastian then heard Liam whisper, "Once you're feeling better, I'm gonna get you out of here. I'm not sure how, yet. But you have to promise to take me with you."

"I promise," Sebastian mumbled.

Chapter Seven

Lying there in the dark, Sebastian's mind filled with thoughts. Still mourning the loss of his dad and sister, tears stung his eyes when wishing they were still alive and all three of them safe at home in Alaska. Since their funeral, his feelings of anger toward his dad for once more abandoning him tore him apart. He wondered if it was normal to be angry at someone who died, leaving behind loved ones unable to follow, and he wondered how long it would take for the hurt inside him to become less painful to endure.

The fear of returning here to San Gabriel soon pushed his despair aside. As much as he was frightened by the replicates that had tried to kill him, Sebastian also thought about the human villains he'd suffered from. What does it take to turn a person evil? With the Lesterman's, maybe it was grief in losing their son. Lexia's evil might have been driven by greed. But Sebastian knew the real devil walking the face of the Earth, stalking the hallways of San Gabriel, espousing his righteous beliefs while punishing those who fall from his twisted version of grace.

Not wanting to think of terrifying people or of those he loved, Sebastian tried clearing his mind, concentrating on how to escape. Others had tried, and when brought back, were forced to endure the re-indoctrination that he had. And afterwards, when allowed to leave the reflection chamber, their every move was watched. Other boys would spy on them, earning an extra piece of bread or a second ladle of broth. You could always tell who they were simply by how healthy they appeared.

Wondering when he would see Liam again, something he'd not thought of before occurred to him. How did Liam get inside the chamber with him? Knowing the room had no windows and only one door, he wondered if Liam had picked the lock or had stolen the key. The only other possibility was through the air vent. Maybe that's where he found his way in?

Trying to sit up, a sharp pain in his ribs forced him to lay back, his chest heaving to capture his breath. Reaching his quaking arms out, Sebastian tried finding a breeze. Feeling slight coolness to his right fingertips, he rolled over in that direction. The light sensation of a faint puff of air cooled his forehead. Certain of the air vent being close, Sebastian rolled one more time. Finding the air vent, his fingers penetrated through the metal screen covering it. Straining to pull it toward him, the vent screen fell away. Tracing the opening, Sebastian knew he'd never be able to squeeze in. But remembering what Liam looked like, he guessed his new friend could fit inside with room to spare.

Understanding the elders or Bender could show up at any time, Sebastian returned the air vent cover to its rightful place. Then, rolling his body away to the other side of the chamber, he hoped to not draw attention to the vent. Sure enough, a few minutes later, Sebastian heard the door unlock and squinted when light flooded in from the main room.

Helped to his feet by Lucas and Jaxson, their demeanor toward him had noticeably altered. "Good morning, Sebastian," Lucas said. "We brought you a new shirt and socks. You should probably take a shower before breakfast. Come on."

Steadied by both of them while being lead out of the reflection chamber, Sebastian saw many of the boys getting dressed and talking amongst them. None paid any attention to him, at least no one he saw. But he knew the spies were there, watching.

"Today's a special day," Jaxson commented. "It's my eighteenth birthday!"

Understanding what was expected, Sebastian responded, "Happy birthday, brother. And thank you for helping me return to the righteous path. You, as well, brother Lucas."

"It's good to have you back, Sebastian," Lucas commented.

Enjoying a somewhat warm shower, Sebastian then dressed and joined the other boys in the cafeteria for breakfast. Hand trembling over his bowl of paste-like oatmeal, he found a seat at the far end of a metal table. After the blessing, Bender appeared, standing next to Jaxson. Expressing his usual false smile, Bender offered his thoughts for this day. "Boys, today we celebrate Jaxson's eighteenth birthday, a rite of passage here. Off into the world he will go, to live a life of purity, to be a light of hope to those suffering. Jaxson has chosen the path of a missionary and will be traveling to our brother home in Nicaragua. Wish him well as he spreads our word to this troubled world."

An eruption of applause followed Benders words. When seated at the table, Jaxson was presented with an extravagant breakfast awarded only to those turning eighteen. Platefuls of pancakes, eggs, sausage, bacon, potatoes, and pastries were set before him. Taking a deep breath, he then picked up his fork and began eating. As customary, no one else would eat until he finished every bite. Yet something unexpected happened, tarnishing the spirit of this celebration.

"He stole food! I saw it! He stole food! He is a thief!" a boy sitting near Jaxon bellowed while pointing at Lucas.

"What is the meaning of this?" Bender questioned when approaching them. Glaring at Lucas, Bender demanded, "Show me your hands."

With his cheeks flushed and swallowing deep, Lucas raised his hands that were at rest in his lap. Turning them over, revealing his empty palms, Bender reached down, forcing Lucas's right hand up to his nose. Deeply inhaling, with an expression brimming with disgust, Bender released his hand. "Was the sausage to your liking?" he asked Lucas, while not looking at him.

"Yes sir," Lucas quietly uttered.

"I can explain," Jaxon attempted to interject, but fell silent when Bender held up his hand.

"No explanation is necessary. Lucas stole food from your plate, shaming himself before his brothers," Bender announced to all.

"No, sir," Jaxson firmly denied. "I gave Lucas the sausage." Recognizing the fear now cast across Lucas's face due to Jaxson's blatant contradiction of Bender, Sebastian knew punishment for both would be forthcoming.

"I see," Bender responded. Appearing thoughtful for a moment, he then suggested, "I should think you would wish to share *more* of your breakfast with Lucas." And with all eyes drawn to the empty plates, he quietly demanded, "Now."

Seeming to understand what was being demanded of him, Jaxson opened his mouth, placing three of his fingers to the back of his throat in forcing himself to gag. Coughing several times, a small amount of undigested breakfast spewed from his throat onto the plate in front of him. As Jaxson's drool covered chin quivered, Bender offered further instruction. "Now, Lucas, please take Jaxson's plate and eat that which he is sharing with you."

Timid in taking the plate, Lucas picked up his spoon and was about to take a bite when Bender stopped him. "Not with a spoon. *Animals* feast with only their mouths when fed table scraps." Taking the plate, Bender set it down on the floor. "Breakfast is served." Easing off his chair, on his hands and knees, Lucas lowered his face to the plate and ate every bite, licking the plate clean as would be expected.

Addressing the other boys, Bender smiled again, saying, "All of you may now eat your breakfast" before taking what remained of Jaxson's breakfast and walking away.

***

Rituals of departure for boys turning eighteen normally call for several moments of celebration, spread throughout the day. Yet due to Jaxson and Lucas disregarding the sanctity of the birthday breakfast, all other customs were suspended. Sebastian couldn't blame them for what they did. From what he'd been told by others, Jaxson and Lucas arrived at San Gabriel on the same day when they were six years old. Bonding over the years, they truly had become brothers in every sense of the word, with exception of sharing the same blood. But from the moment breakfast ended, Bender saw to the breaking of their bond. Lucas was placed in the reflection chamber, with the promise of being released once Jaxson had left. They would have no chance of saying goodbye to each other.

Having found an unoccupied top bunk to lay on, Sebastian stared at the light flooding through the dirty windows in the main room. Clinging to the stagnant air was a haze of dust, making it seem as if traces of smoke from a nearby fire. That thought appealed to him, of an inferno burning San Gabriel to the ground. He imagined the forest fire he'd lived through in Canada reaching the shelter and pictured Bender as one of the replicate soldiers, melting to nothing from the extreme heat and flames.

Glancing up at the rafters and the corrugated-steel ceiling, he noticed a network of round exposed ducts and air shafts with one vent directly high up over top his bed. While not really focused on it, from the corner of his eye he thought he saw a white shadow piercing the darkness inside the vent. Thinking for a moment, Sebastian tried hiding his smile when thinking Liam might be prowling above.

To his surprise, a stick of gum wrapped in silver, fell onto his chest. Although knowing it was a gift from Liam, he worried that one of the spies might have seen it drop. Needing to be rid of it, Sebastian tossed the gum onto the top bunk across from his. And to further divert suspicion from him, he pointed to a boy two beds over. When becoming aware of Sebastian wanting his attention, his eyes followed Sebastian's pointed finger to the bunk between them. Seeing what lay there, the boy shouted out, "How did he get gum? I bet he stole it from Mister Bender!"

Unknown to Sebastian, the bunk belonged to the boy who'd told on Jaxson and Lucas. He'd received a partially rotten apple for his reward in exposing the two elders. Now he was the one being exposed, although innocent of this crime. "That's not mine!" he strongly denied. But his denial and protest were soon drowned out when several boys loudly dragged him away, seeking out Bender's harsh punishment for him. Although wanting to feel sorry for the boy, just knowing he was also a spy robbed Sebastian of sympathy. Then it occurred to him what was really happening. By further engaging in the savagery of survival tactics here in San Gabriel, his soul drew nearer to the brink of being lost. Filled with regret in framing the boy, faintly under his breath he mumbled, "I have to get away from here, before it's too late."

Chapter Eight

Rolling over, Sebastian awoke to snoring, heard from several directions. Burying his head under his pillow to try and drowned out the sound, he felt a tug at the bottom of his blanket. Sitting up, his eyes were drawn to a trail of blue glowing dots on his blanket. When spying over the edge of his bed, he saw more blue dots leading away from his bunk.

Carefully climbing down, hoping not to wake anyone, he padded barefoot on the cold floor, following the dots toward the bathroom. Paranoid with fear of being seen by the spies, before leaving the main room, Sebastian crouched down low, keeping still while listening. Hearing no movements, he continued on, thankful that the door glided open with no sounds.

Entering the bathroom, the blue dots led Sebastian to the farthest stall where the trail ended. Bending down, he glanced under the stall door, seeing no feet. But before he could touch the door to push it in, it silently opened, revealing Liam's hiding place. His friend's welcoming smile caused him to exhale with relief.

"Where did you get that glowing blue stuff?" Sebastian asked while stepping into the stall and closing the door behind him.

"From this," Liam answered, holding out a long tube with just a little glowing blue stuff inside. "I think it's called a *glow stick*. I stole a whole pack of them when I was out last night. There's red, yellow, and blue."

Looking at his friend, Sebastian said, "I'm glad you're safe."

"You, too," Liam responded with a big grin. "Listen, we don't have much time. I found a way for you to get out."

"Where?"

Pointing up to the air vent, Liam revealed, "This vent is different from the others. It's bigger and leads straight up to the roof. There are even rungs inside, like a ladder."

"So what are we waiting for?" Sebastian asked, ready to climb on the toilet to reach the vent.

"Stop!" Liam urged, holding Sebastian's arm. "We don't have enough time. Sunrise is in just a few minutes. I can't be outside anymore. We have to wait until tonight."

"Okay. We'll wait until midnight. By then everyone else should be asleep." The disappointment on his face must have been noticeable.

"I promise, *tonight*, we'll both be out of here for good," Liam reassured him.

"I just gotta get away from here," Sebastian mumbled.

Grabbing his trembling hand, Liam said, "Stop being so nervous. We're going to be okay, *really*!" Not wanting to tell his friend about his Parkinson's disease, Sebastian faked his best smile, though feeling anxious and worried inside that something was going to go wrong.

Hearing the door to the bathroom open, Sebastian placed his finger to his lips and motioned that he was going to step out of the stall. Closing the door behind him, Sebastian looked down at the floor, seeing that the blue dots were no longer glowing, seeming to have disappeared. He walked over to the sink and turned on the faucet. Filling his palms with cold water, he splashed his face as Lucas came around the corner.

"You're up early," Lucas commented.

"The snoring woke me up. I couldn't fall back to sleep." Lucas smile while nodding his head in understanding. "Well, I should go get dressed."

"Hold on," Lucas stopped him, appearing kind of nervous. "Can I talk to you for a minute?"

"Sure."

Leaning back against a faded-blue tile wall, Lucas asked, "Did you see Jaxson leave yesterday?"

"No. I saw him sitting alone before dinner but after that I didn't see him again."

Near tears, Lucas burst out, "I didn't get to say goodbye to him!"

Feeling sorry for him, Sebastian commented, "Well, maybe once you leave here someday, you could meet up with him. *Maybe* you could go to Nicaragua to be a missionary too.

Stepping close to Sebastian, Lucas whispered, "I don't think that will happen."

"Why not?"

Still keeping his voice low, Lucas continued, "Because I have a bad feeling he didn't go to Nicaragua."

"Where did he go?"

"I don't know. When Bender left me alone in his office for almost a half hour about a week ago, I was kind of snooping around. I couldn't find anything about missionaries or Nicaragua. I looked through his desk drawers and even looked on his computer. *Nothing*."

"Well, where would he have gone then?"

"I don't know, but there was one thing I did find, or actually *didn't* find."

"What?"

"I knew three boys who turned eighteen last year. Their files are missing. I overheard Bender telling social services that the files of all the boys are kept for five years."

"So he keeps them in a different place," Sebastian tried reasoning.

"I don't think so," Lucas responded. From his pocket, he pulled out some shreds of paper. Putting them together in his palm, as if a puzzle, they spelled a name. "I accidentally tripped over his paper shredder and found this underneath. Michael was one of the boys who left last year. I'm sure this was from his file."

Not knowing what to think of this, Sebastian said, "I don't know what to say."

"Can I trust you not to say anything about this?" Lucas asked.

"Say anything about *what*?" Sebastian answered and then walked away. Checking the clock on the wall when stepping back into the main room, he knew the next sixteen hours might be the longest of his life. All he needed to do was to survive until midnight.

***

Mindful of an old saying about watched clocks never moving, Sebastian spent much of the day either trying to sleep, playing basketball during outdoor time, or squinting without his glasses at the small print of a book Bender had written years ago, the only book allowed at San Gabriel. Outlining his philosophies of righteousness and distorting religious facts in formulating his doctrine, Bender's rhetoric would have been considered blasphemous to most religious scholars. Discarding it after reading three paragraphs, Sebastian was content with not being able to see all the words.

Another thing achieved during the day was purposely avoiding Lucas. Several times, Sebastian fell under the elder boy's stare, and while he'd thought about Lucas's suspicions regarding Jaxson and other boys whom had left, in the end what happened to them mattered little to him. Truth be told, he was happy they were gone.

Light's out came at ten o'clock. For the next hour, the sounds of restless boys and whispered chatter kept him alert. Several times, with his patience growing thin, he wanted to yell out for them to shut up. But by eleven-thirty, practically all the sounds had ceased, with several boys loudly snoring. And once the hands on the clock reached midnight, the time for escape was at hand.

As silent as possible, Sebastian climbed down the bunk, ever cautious not to alert any spies whose sleep might be light or restless. Having left his San Gabriel shirt behind, a chill in the air caused him to tremble. When reaching the door to the bathroom, he hoped the tremors coursing through his hands would allow him to grip the doorknob without causing noise. As he had done in the morning, before leaving the main room, he crouched down low, checking one last time for watchful spies.

Stepping into the bathroom, he kept the lights dim and snuck over to the last stall. Once inside, he noticed that the overhead air vent cover had been left open. Climbing up onto the toilet, he teetered for a moment before finding his balance. Sebastian expected Liam to be there waiting for him, but there was no sign of his friend. Reaching up into the dark air shaft, he felt the ladder rungs Liam told him about. Guessing that Liam was waiting for him on the roof, Sebastian gripped the rungs, pulling himself up with his feet dangling. Stretching his left hand up, he soon found the next rung to grasp.

Once fully inside the air shaft, Sebastian continued climbing. Stopping a few times, listening for sounds from below, being sure he hadn't been heard, he continued up. By the time he reached the top of the rungs, his hands cramped from the tremors. Stretching his arm up, Sebastian discovered the rooftop cover, but nearly lost his hold of the rung, realizing that something had jammed it shut from the inside. Feeling around, he guessed it might be a metal pipe wedged through the handle and across the frame. The pipe failed to budge when pulled, but by twisting it, he was successful in unjamming the cover.

Heavy in weight, he pressed hard against the metal cover until he was able to slip out. Lowering down onto the rooftop, Sebastian's heart throbbed when finding his friend lying there. His eyes exploded with fear, seeing that Liam's arm had been chained to a pipe, leaving him only able to touch the air vent cover, but too far away to slip inside.

Crawling over to him, Sebastian choked out, *"Liam?"*

Panting with shallow breaths, Liam turned his head toward Sebastian. *"You made it. I knew you would,"* he faintly uttered.

Scooting close to him, Sebastian dragged Liam onto his lap, holding his shuddering, overheated body. Bathed in brilliant moonlight, the entire rooftop was aglow as if just before sunset. Glancing down, Sebastian's heart broke, seeing how scorched and blistered his friend's chest, arms, and face appeared. Stripped of his shirt, his hands felt like they were being roasted by the heat radiating from Liam's skin.

"Who did this to you?" Sebastian whispered, unable to hold back his tears. He already knew the answer and it enraged him when hearing it.

"Bender," Liam answered. Sebastian then fell apart when Liam said, "I can't come with you."

"Yes, you can. I'll find something to free you," Sebastian said, wiping his tears away.

"No. You have to go."

"I can't leave you. Tell me what I can do?" Sebastian uttered while pulling Liam closer.

But Liam clearly grew disoriented, not responding to Sebastian's question but asking his own. "Is that the sun?" he wondered when pointing into the night sky. "It's really pretty."

Swallowing, Sebastian answered, "No, that's the moon." And as Liam took his final breath, Sebastian whispered, "But some like to call it the midnight sun."

Part Two

Nightfall

Chapter Nine

Kissing Liam's forehead, Sebastian whispered, "I'm sorry. I waited too long to get here." Gently resting his friend's body down on the roof, he turned away, struggling in gasping for his breath. Then, managing to stand, feeling light-headed, he closed his eyes. The throbbing of his heart seemed to match the racing of his pulse.

Alerted by the sounds of someone climbing the air shaft, Sebastian staggered back. Losing his balance, he stumbled over the ledge, falling down off the roof. Falling in slow motion, dragging out what he thought would be his death, the pain felt when slamming hard on top of plastic trash bags jarred him from this suspended moment. Further winded by the impact, Sebastian quickly wondered if he would ever breathe again.

Furiously panting, the air his lungs captured rushed from his body when finding a hand near his cheek. Fearfully rolling away, a trash bag spilled over, uncovering Jaxson's pale, lifeless face. With his mind racing to understand what he'd found, the sounds of an approaching garbage truck echoed from the other end of the alley. Clawing his way out of the dumpster, Sebastian was able to climb out with a minute to spare before the dumpster was lifted and unloaded.

Overwhelmed by sadness and fear, Sebastian wandered away, unable to focus his mind on anything with his eyes vacantly staring away.

***

"Is there anything else?" Lexia asked, tracing her long fingernail around the brim of her coffee cup.

Checking her electronic table, her secretary, Fiona, answered, "Just two more. The additional security measures here at One Legacy Place, as well as your apartment in the city, have been implemented as per your instructions."

"Excellent," Lexia responded before sipping her coffee.

"And finally, an update from the Bay Area Missing Child's database. The boy you've been searching for was found by the police."

"Where?" Lexia asked, attempting to mask her surprise.

"He was found wandering in a park near the Mission District, here in San Francisco."

"Here in the *city?*" Believing he was in Alaska, his being found so close startled her. She'd never imagined he would return.

"Are you alright?" Fiona asked.

"I'm fine," she lied.

"Do you know him?"

Pausing for a moment, she answered, "I am acquainted with his mother."

After taking another sip of her coffee, Lexia calmly instructed, "Find out where he is. Make this your priority."

"Certainly," Fiona confirmed before leaving.

***

A few hours later while standing just out of sight, she overheard a conversation between two police officers at the Mission District Police Precinct.

"Yeah, I found him around two this morning, completely incoherent. He seems to be coming around, though. I got him to drink some milk about an hour ago. Poor kid."

"Did he say anything to you?"

"No. I think he's too scared."

"Do you think he's on drugs?"

"I'm sure he's not. Look at the cuts all over his face. And under the t-shirt we gave him, his chest and stomach are covered with bruises. It's obvious the kid was abused. And get this, after matching his picture on the missing kids database, I found out that he's from the San Gabriel Boys Shelter. They reported him missing months ago."

"That place is a crap hole. The guy running it is a maniac. Did you call him?"

"No, not yet. I want to talk to the captain first. He's been in briefings all morning. I called the hospital for a psych evaluation. They can't get anyone down here until later this afternoon."

Hearing her chance, Lexia walked up to the two officers. "Hello, I'm Madeline Richards. I'm here for the psychiatric evaluation," she lied.

"Wow, you're here a lot sooner than I thought you would be," the first officer commented.

"Children take a priority," she responded with a smile.

"Where's your briefcase?" the second officer asked.

"I don't wish to frighten him. I prefer keeping it informal, just talking at first."

"I should probably ask for your identification or credentials," the first officer said.

Charming the officer with her smile, Lexia replied, "Both are in my briefcase. Would it be alright if I presented you with them later? I think this young man should be our immediate priority. Don't you agree?"

"That will be fine," the first officer answered. "Let's go in."

Hesitating, she lowered her voice, saying, "With both of us going in, he might be too overwhelmed or frightened to talk. I should talk to him alone."

"I don't know. I have to follow procedures."

"I assure you I'll be fine and will alert you if needed."

Thinking it over for a moment, the officer relented. "Okay."

When entering the room, Lexia noticed a quick glance from Sebastian to her. Offering no reaction, he looked away as she sat opposite him at the table. After a minute of deafening silence, she was about to say something but he spoke first. "Did you come to kill me?"

Nervously exhaling, Lexia replied, "To be honest, I'm not sure why I'm here."

Placing his trembling hands on the table in front of him, Sebastian confirmed for her, "Dad and Lydy are dead."

Growing more uncomfortable with every second, Lexia uttered, "I know." She attempted to smile, remarking, "I like that you called her Lydy. That's what I called her, when we were alone together."

"W-why are you here?" he struggled to say. "I don't see how you can punish me more than you already have."

Unsure of what to say, Lexia just stared at him. By his forlorn expression, she recognized how the deep sadness and torment he must be reeling from had left him vulnerable, almost to the point of destroying him. His soft grey eyes were so revealing of his devastation. Unable to stop herself, she whispered, "You remind me *so much* of your father. You have his eyes."

After saying this, her last words stuck in her mind with an impossible thought growing. Echoing her words, once more she whispered, "You have his eyes." Abruptly pulling her smart phone from the pocket of her black trench coat, she began typing on the small keyboard, drawing Sebastian's attention.

"What are you doing?"

"Hopefully saving us both," Lexia mumbled. Stopping for a moment, she returned her attention to Sebastian, looking thoughtfully at him. Then leaning forward, she spoke under her breath. "I need your help with something. Please."

"I don't understand."

"I know of a way to stop *Nightfall* but only with your help."

"Why would I want to stop it?"

"Because there's a target on both our backs. Do you really think the car crash that killed your father and Lydia was an *accident*? Listen to me. There are those who will stop at nothing to disable the *Nightfall* security breach your father created. And they will kill anyone they believe are connected to it. You and I are the only two left."

Appearing lost to his thoughts, Sebastian then caught her off guard by asking, "Tell me about when I was taken away from my dad and mom."

"We don't have time for that."

"Make time," Sebastian insisted.

Drawn in by the sadness of his eyes, Lexia thought of her response, revealing enough but keeping some parts hidden. "I found out that Lydia had hired someone to abduct you. The man contacted me, saying that if I didn't pay him a hundred thousand dollars more then he would expose both of us with conspiracy to kidnap a child. When I went to Boston to pay him, I found him dead and you unharmed. I wanted to protect my daughter, and myself, so I took you to a homeless shelter and bribed a man to take you and never reveal where you came from."

"Did you inject me with Parkinson's disease?"

Unnerved by his unexpected question, the word "yes" breathlessly escaped her lips. Remembering that night, in truth she'd made a careless mistake. Having injected him with wrong syringe, had she not made this error, Sebastian would have died from genetically enhanced Pneumonia.

"Why?"

Swallowing hard, she answered, "I was angry at your father and wanted to destroy him."

"I guess you got what you wanted."

Leaning back, she corrected him. "No, it wasn't what I wanted. I just couldn't stop myself." Guardedly reaching over, she covered Sebastian's tremoring hands with hers. "I can't undo what I've done. I deserve nothing less than your hatred. But this, stopping *Nightfall*, is one thing I can do, but not without you."

Seeming confused, Sebastian asked, "How could I be of any help to you? I only know enough about computers to get by. And I don't know anything about *Nightfall*. Dad and I really didn't talk about it."

"Your father kept a special lab at One Legacy Place. He designed it with impenetrable walls and door and with a unique security system, which only allowed him to enter. I've tried everything I could think of to gain entry. But your father was brilliant. In designing protection for his lab, he anticipated every attempt I would make in trying to get in."

"I still don't understand how I can help you."

"Have you ever heard the term *doppelganger*?"

"No."

"It means *twin* or *mirror image*. That's what *you* are, especially your eyes. You have your father's eyes. *That* is how we gain access to your father's private lab."

"My *eyes*?"

"Yes. Your father knew how unique his eyes were. There were microscopic specks of silver floating in his eyes and I believe in yours, as well. Understanding how this could not artificially be duplicated, he designed his labs security to only open the door with retinal and cornea recognition, a simple eye scan."

"So, if I agree to allow my eyes to be scanned and the door opens, then what happens?"

"Then I can terminate the *Nightfall* data breach."

"And after that, are you gonna kill me?"

"No."

"Why not?"

A part of her wanted to tell him about her being his biological mother, but she knew he'd never believe it. Pulling her hands back and looking into her palms, she answered, "Because I don't want to hurt you. I can't explain it. Please don't ask me to try."

Piercingly staring at her, Sebastian glanced toward the door. "I'm pretty sure we can't just walk out of here. Bender's probably waiting to take me back to the shelter."

Regaining her composure, Lexia commented, "Neither will be a problem." Again she began typing on her smart phone's keyboard. "You father wasn't the only computer genius. Prepare yourself, things are about to get wet."

With the press of a button, the fire alarm began blaring and the overhead sprinklers turned on, drenching them both. Hearing the commotion outside, they rushed to the door. Stepping out, the first police officer she spoke to motioned for them to go to the right, ushering them out of the building.

In the midst of the ensuing chaos while leading Sebastian away from the police precinct, an unfamiliar man approached them. Halting his steps, Sebastian stood quaking with noticeable fear when the man smiled. "*Sebastian*, I was worried about you. I came as soon as I heard you were found."

"And *who* are you?" Lexia asked.

"Oh, my apology. I'm Darrin Bender, administrator of the San Gabriel Boys Shelter."

From a pocket on her trench coat, Lexia withdrew a small handgun. Pointing it at Bender, she shot him in the head before he could blink. "Another problem solved," she commented while stepping over his dead body.

Stunned by what she'd done, Lexia dragged Sebastian away by his hand. Approaching her sleek black Mercedes, the doors unlocked, opening up like the wings of a bird. "Get in." Once seated, through voice-activation she commanded, "One Legacy Place."

Chapter Ten

"You're welcome," Sebastian heard Lexia say to him. Shocked from watching her kill Bender, he could barely think straight while wondering if it was even right to be thankful for what she'd done for him. But the one thing Sebastian knew for certain was that he'd sold his soul to the devil and there was no turning back.

With the fog lifting from his thoughts, he finally said, "Thank you."

"Was he the one who beat you?"

"No, he told some older boys to do it," Sebastian answered, leaning his head against the window. With her car maneuvering through traffic, he stared out the window at the San Francisco skyline, a world he once knew turned violently upside down. He came back here to reclaim the life he once had, but the old saying held true. You can never go home. So where do you go? How do you find the courage to seek out a new place in the world, especially if you're alone?

"You didn't ask me what I thought would have been an obvious question," Lexia commented after a few silent minutes.

Continuing to look away from her, Sebastian asked, "What question would that be?"

"If I had anything to do with the car crash in Alaska that killed your father and sister."

"Did you?"

"No."

Silence resumed between them. Watching as they veered off the highway onto a ramp leading into a well-lit underground tunnel, he could barely feel the car moving. But just a short ways in, with the flickering of the interior car lights, their smooth ride came to a halt. Appearing drained of power, Lexia tried both voice-activation and manual override, with neither action proving capable of re-starting the car. And in the following minutes, the lights in the tunnel dimmed and then went out, plunging all around them into pitch blackness.

Using her smart phone, Lexia called her secretary. "Fiona, my car has stopped in the Corvellis Tunnel. Are we experiencing an outage?"

After a short pause, Fiona responded, "A power surge has disrupted the transportation grid you were driving in. All other grids seem to be operational."

"Send another car to the Blaine Street entrance for the tunnel." Whispering to Sebastian, Lexia said, "We'll have to walk."

"I'll send a car for you and Sebastian right away."

As soon as Fiona hung up, Lexia sounded panicked. "We need to get out of here, *now*!"

"What's wrong?"

"I never told Fiona you were with me." Pressing against her door, she opened hers just before the all the locks suddenly clicked. "You'll have to get out through my door."

Climbing over her seat, Sebastian felt her reaching for his hand.

"I'm not sure where to go," she uttered, breathing hard while dragging him along.

Thinking about where they were, Sebastian stopped her. "*Wait*! I know this tunnel. I've walked through here before. There's an emergency stairwell up there on the left. *Come on*!" Leading her farther into the tunnel, they slowed their pace when hearing engine sounds approaching. "*Hurry*!" he then urged her on.

Running their hands along the cement wall, they found a metal door. Pulling on it, at first it seemed stuck, but when trying again, it opened just enough for them both to squeeze through. Closing it behind them most of the way, leaving only a sliver to see through, Sebastian saw rapid flashes of light accompanied by shots fired from guns. "Come on. I'm not waiting for them to find us." Climbing metal circular stairs lit by a shaft of sunlight from the above opening, when reaching the top, Sebastian motioned for her to follow him down an alley to the left.

"Where are we going? We need to get to One Legacy Place," Lexia reminded him.

Stopping, he turned to her. "Isn't that where Fiona is?"

Exhaling, Lexia leaned back against a brick wall. "Yes, of course. I'm not thinking straight. I need to come up with a plan."

"We should disappear for a while. I know of a place a couple blocks away from here. If we stick to the alleys, we should get there with no problem." Passing through shaded alleys on their way to his hiding place, Sebastian tried to avoid looking at the dumpsters, not wanting to think about finding Jaxson's body or reliving his last minutes with Liam.

After climbing several flights up a fire escape, Sebastian and Lexia arrived at his rooftop refuge. "What is this place?" Lexia asked, both confused and mildly appalled.

When walking over to the utility room door, Sebastian answered, "This is where I live."

"You can't be serious."

Brushing off her comment, he offered, "You can come in, if you want." Seeing her step in the doorway, he felt uncomfortable by how she stared in. "Not everyone's rich like you," Sebastian defended his home.

"I never meant to offend you," Lexia apologized. Appearing thoughtful, she commented, "I see that you must be an avid reader by all the books you have."

"Yeah, I like to read."

"So do I. Charles Dickens is my favorite author. I could never get your father to read anything. He was always too busy with his work. He loved music, though."

"Journey was his favorite rock group, especially the songs on *Frontiers*."

"Yes," Lexi agreed. "I wasn't certain you knew that."

"That's all he listened to when we were at the lighthouse. I like them too."

Feeling light-headed, Sebastian staggered, falling back onto his cot.

"Are you alright?" Lexia sounded concerned.

Closing his eyes, he answered, "It'll pass in a minute. I'll be fine." Reaching out his tremoring hand, when trying to grab his glasses, they slipped from his fingers and fell to the floor. Before he could retrieve them, Lexia had bent down to get them for him.

"Here."

"Thanks."

After putting them on, Sebastian noticed how oddly Lexia was staring at him. Felling uncomfortable, he asked, "What?"

"I'm sorry. It's just that you remind me so much of your father. Your voice even sounds similar to his. I don't mean to upset you by saying that."

"It's okay."

Sighing, Lexia then suggested, "You know, after *Nightfall* is disabled, you won't have to live like this anymore. You're the heir to a billion-dollar empire. You could live anywhere you want to and have anything your heart desires."

Feeling sad when thinking of what he most wanted, Sebastian quietly responded, "No."

"Why would you refuse something like that?"

Deflecting her question, he remarked, "It doesn't matter. I won't be coming back here again."

Clearly startled, she asked, "Where will you go?"

"I don't know."

Seeming frustrated by his response, he watched as Lexia turned away from him, leaning against the door frame while looking out at the afternoon sky. Wanting both to break the awkward silence and move on with things, Sebastian asked, "So how do we get in to One Legacy Place?"

***

Huddled together, looking at the computer screen in an internet café a few blocks from One Legacy Place, Lexia pulled up structural schematics of the tower. Quietly, she revealed, "With recent security upgrades, it will prove much more difficult for us to enter unnoticed. *Difficult—* but not impossible."

"So, you have a back door," Sebastian commented.

"No, not exactly a back door, but I know of a secure way to get to your father's lab."

"Where is it?"

Enlarging the screen, Lexia pointed to a stairwell near the core of the tower. "This shaft is used primarily by maintenance workers. There's a mixture of ladders, elevators and steps leading to the towers pointed top."

"Are you kidding me? Right in the middle of the tower? Does it at least have an entrance in the underground parking garage?"

Slightly shaking her head no, she answered, "No. We'll need to walk passed the main bank of elevators to reach it."

"Meaning that we'll have to walk through the front door."

"Passed the armed guards standing outside, through the atrium, metal detectors, and additional guards near the information desk," she added.

"How are we going to get passed all that?"

"Just like you said, by walking through the front door," Lexia hesitantly revealed.

"*Seriously!* We're just going to walk through the front door. They're going to be waiting for you. Everyone knows who you are."

"I own the company. *Of course* they know who I am."

"And you're not worried they'll shoot you as you walk in? What am I missing?"

"Listen to me. Fear has its privileges," she explained. "Practically everyone who works for me cowers like frightened children in my presence. I run Dryden Technologies with an iron fist. Most, if not all, will avoid either looking at me or talking to me, acting as if I have the plague. I've terminated employees simply because I didn't like the expression on their faces or the clothing they wore."

"I guess that makes sense," Sebastian sarcastically remarked. "And what about the guards?"

"If they truly want to murder me, they won't kill me in such a public setting. There would be too many witnesses. I suspect they would wait until I reached my office or one of the conference rooms. Then they would have more options in *how* to kill me, making my death look like a suicide and caused by a small tragic explosion in claiming my life."

"So, what's to stop them from coming after you in the maintenance stairwell?"

"There's only three ways in. One through my office, which can only be voice activated, one through your father's lab, which hopefully will open when scanning your eyes, and the lobby door near the elevators, which I will lock behind us, again, through voice activation."

"Won't they get in by using maintenance access codes?"

"I can simply override them. That will buy us enough time to get into your father's lab."

"*Awesome!*" Sebastian mockingly commented. "When do we go?"

"As soon as we buy some new clothes," Lexia answered. "After all, we'll be walking through the social elite, and I always make an entrance."

***

Wearing a thousand-dollar white V-neck t-shirt under an all-white varsity jacket and black jeans and sneakers, Sebastian forced the thought of how much his clothes cost aside while following Lexia into the One Legacy Place plaza. Informing him of how retro was the current fashion trend, she'd purchased for herself a vintage-inspired black and white skirt and jacket with a matching wide brimmed hat, appearing as if stepping off the Hollywood silver screen.

"People are staring at us," Sebastian mumbled under his breath.

Glancing about, Lexia soon ended her employee's curious and careless gazes.

"Are you sure this is going to work?"

"Of course," Lexia replied. "Arriving is the easy part."

"What about leaving?"

"I haven't figured that out yet."

Chapter Eleven

When approaching the main tower doors, Sebastian noticed that he and Lexia had drawn the attention of the outside security guards. He also observed how they all shared the same face, revealing each one in being a replicate. Too scared to comment on this, he walked closer to Lexia as they entered the building.

The glass atrium appeared as impressive as it did the first time he stepped in One Legacy Place. He clearly remembered the illuminated fountains, the polished marble floors, and massive modern art sculptures and paintings. There was, however, a striking new addition to the décor, an even larger brushed-silver statue spiked at its top, reminiscent of the building itself.

Lexia's claim that employees feared her seemed false when seeing several stop dead in their tracks, their eyes holding firm to her. Glancing back, Sebastian saw a number of the guards from outside entering the building. And as they approached the metal detectors, the conversations of those at the information desk ceased. Sebastian wished he had a pin, knowing he'd hear it if dropping it. "Do they act this way every time you enter?"

"No," she answered quietly.

Passing through the metal detectors, Sebastian followed Lexia to the farthest elevator. Seeing the maintenance door to their right, he wondered why she'd pressed the elevator button. Spying out the corner of his eye, he saw several of the replicate guards gathering near the metal detectors, keeping them both in their sights. Turning away, he heard her say, "Priority override, access Lexia Dryden."

To his surprise, the maintenance door swung open. Dragging him by his hand, they just barely got inside the maintenance shaft as the ricochet of a bullet sparked against the metal door. Tossing her hat and kicking off her high-heels, her voice echoed, "Follow me."

Climbing several steps, before reaching the first landing, the ear-splitting sounds of the building's fire alarm blared down the maintenance shaft, heightening Sebastian's fear. Stumbling behind her, Lexia took hold of his hand, leading him up several more flights of stairs, before reaching the eighth floor, Light-headed and disoriented, Sebastian fell down, nearly hyperventilating, his eyes shifting from side-to-side, trying to regain focus. Gripping his jacket, he attempted to pull it off, but the tremors in his hands wouldn't let him.

"Just two more flights!" he heard Lexia's voice over the alarm. Assisting him in pulling off his jacket, she then helped him to his feet as they continued on. Each step grew more difficult for him to climb with Sebastian leaning on her for the final two. There in front of them, on the tenth-floor landing, appeared a solid metal door and a video monitor set off to the left.

Heard over the alarm, a monotone male voice instructed, "Please step up to the control panel for eye scan confirmation." Helping position him before the monitor, Lexia then stepped back. The bright light from a laser then appeared, scanning Sebastian's open eyes. A seemingly endless minute passed before the voice spoke again. "Eye scan confirmation verified." Both their jaws dropped with shock when the door slid open, revealing an elevator.

Stepping inside, the elevator door immediately closed after them, Sebastian said, "I thought this would be his lab."

"So did I," Lexia agreed.

"Destination, please." the male monotone voice requested.

Tracing her finger down a listing of floor options, Lexia commented, "I never knew this elevator existed. It's not on any of the schematics." Deeply exhaling, she continued, "And neither is this." Speaking clear, she instructed, "Subterranean level four."

Both then heard, "Voice authorization denied. Please select again."

Remembering her earlier comment regarding his voice, Sebastian instructed, "Subterranean Level four."

Following a short pause, they both heard, "Voice authorization confirmed." Then under his feet, he felt the subtle sensation of the elevator descending, with it coming to a halt after a few minutes. "Subterranean level four. Please exit."

The elevator door silently opened to a dark space. But when stepping out, overhead lights lit the lab, revealing several work stations, smart boards covered with notations and complex mathematic equations, and blinking rows of what appeared to be a super computer. At the lab's center sat a frosted-glass desk with a chair and a white laptop computer.

Appearing overwhelmed, Lexia whispered, "Thank you, Sebastian," as she wandered further into his dad's lab.

Following her to what he believed was his dad's desk, Sebastian spied over Lexia's shoulder when she sat down. Rather than attempting to type in the required password, he watched as her fingers glided over the keyboard without pressing anything, as if confused in searching for something. "This could take a while," she mumbled.

Stepping back, curious over this hidden part of his dad's life, Sebastian slowly walked away. Glancing here and there, part of the lab reminded him of a teen hangout space featuring an old couch, a pinball machine, and two posters decorating the wall: a movie poster from the film *Tron* and the album cover for Journey's *Frontiers*. The rest of the lab reminded him of a control room usually shown in science fiction movies, possibly the helm of a starship. A wall of video monitors also reminded him of the control room from the train in Canada. With all the screens blank, for a moment he wondered what they would reveal until they all unexpectedly turned on in unison. Feeling his heart reach his throat and the air rush from his lungs, Sebastian called out to Lexia, "You need to see this."

***

"What are you watching?" Scotty asked when sitting down on the sofa next to his dad.

"A live news feed from San Francisco," Abdul answered. "It seems that not *only* has General Reddinger come out of hiding, but she has also been fully exonerated of all charges against her in connection with the replicate crisis. With the President's full support, General Reddinger is spearheading all efforts to bring Lexia Dryden to justice. Evidence provided by the general, contradicting what was released in the *Nightfall* data breach, implicates Lexia in masterminding the international synthetic replicate conspiracy. And as we speak, government forces have surrounded One Legacy Place, where Lexia was seen entering only a short while ago."

"Do you think she's guilty?"

"*Of course,* she is. Yet a scheme with such magnitude could never have been achieved by the sole efforts of one. Yes, she is to blame, but she had to have help. And from what I understand of Lee's *Nightfall* data breach, with such accuracy of detail, General Reddinger should never have been found innocent of charges against her."

"Meaning that she's still guilty in her part of this?"

"Correct."

"Then why would the President lie and support her?"

Exhaling deep, Abdul responded, "Either the President is lying or those behind the President are conspiring for any number of reasons. What you should understand is that the government has been systematically telling lies for centuries, be it driven by just cause or political ambition. Trust in government is no more than well formulated deception in inducing the masses to blindly follow."

"That's kind of a bleak view of government," Scotty commented.

"I learned my cynicism as a teenager growing up in Aleppo, in Syria during the civil war. Leaders from all sides told lies to achieve their goals."

"Is that why you left?"

"Yes. I was given the opportunity to come to America with the promise of safety."

"But you weren't safe?"

"No, not at first. Over time, things changed or I found a way to adapt." Resting his hand on Scotty's arm, Abdul smiled and added, "My advice to you is to listen to your heart and your mind. They will never lie to you, unlike the words and actions of others."

***

Stepping over to the wall of video monitors, Lexia saw military support vehicles and tanks positioning around the perimeter of One Legacy Place. Sky views also shone attack helicopters and drones hovering near the tower's upper floors. Not intending to sound sarcastic, she reminded Sebastian, "I told you, I always make an entrance."

"How are you with exits?" he asked.

Ignoring his question, Lexia returned to Lee's desk. Summoning her courage, she began typing every password she could think of to access the information in his laptop computer. After a dozen failed attempts, she pounded on the keyboard in frustration. Reasoning out load, she murmured, "I've tried names and dates and everything even remotely associated to replicates and *Nightfall*. Damn you, what password did you use? I've come too close to fail now."

Startled by Sebastian asking a question, Lexia confusingly asked, "What?"

"The guards outside are replicates. What happened to all the humans the replicates were modeled on?"

"We don't have time to worry about that," she tried brushing off his question.

"Make time! I want to know."

Exhaling her frustration, she revealed, "They were taken to secret Dryden labs around the world." Turning away, she continued, "Most didn't survive. A few got away. Most of those were found and killed."

"*Most?*"

"There was one who got away. We haven't been able to find him."

"What's his name?"

"Why does that matter?"

"It matters to me," Sebastian insisted. "What was his name?"

"You really expect me to know that?"

"Yes, because there's only *one*. What was his name?"

Swallowing hard, Lexia answered, "Officer Bentley Thomas Lesterman, a police officer from Boston. I believe you and your father met his parents." Glancing at Sebastian, she watched him walk away, seeming bewildered.

Closing her eyes, she fought to focus her thoughts on Lee, of anything he would think of as being important. But with the military surrounding the tower and the growing understanding that they may not survive, a sense of hopelessness gripped her. Admitting defeat was never a concept she could handle well, normally sweeping the blame off on someone else. In truth, Lee was the one at fault for everything. Had he not hacked into sensitive data systems and collected damaging information, releasing to both the public and government, she and her collaborators just might have succeeded.

One word passing through her mind suddenly halted her thought process. "Of course, how stupid of me," she uttered. Reaching into her pocket for her cell phone, she pulled up her phone number listing and found the one she most needed. Pressing on it, both the name and number appeared on the screen. Waiting for minute, she finally connected with the one she knew could help her most.

"Hello," a voice answered.

"I need the assistance of a master hacker," Lexia said. "One who's gained impossible accesses before."

"Why would I consider helping you?"

"Do you know where I'm calling from?"

"I have a guess."

"Well then, you might find it interesting to know that Sebastian is here with me."

"You're lying."

"What if I'm not? Are you willing to risk his life disbelieving me?

"He hates you. He'd never be there with you."

"Very well, I'll hang up, and you'll never know for sure if I was telling the truth. Goodbye, Scotty."

"*Wait!*"

Chapter Twelve

Having hoped to forget the hours spent at the Lesterman farm, learning that their son had somehow escaped from one of Dryden's hidden labs brought memories flooding back to Sebastian of those terrible hours spent there. He wondered if Ben would have found his way home and how he'd react when finding his dad lying dead near his replicate and his mom missing. Having lived through a similar circumstance in coming home to his dad and sister gone, Sebastian understood what Ben may have experienced and felt a sense of guilt in what happened there.

Lost to these thoughts, while wandering just past the super computer, Sebastian's eyes were drawn to something he never imagined seeing again. Set in the farthest corner of his dad's lab stood a Daybreak chamber, his dad's sophisticated virtual reality program. Thinking there were only two, the discovery of another both excited and scared him at the same time, leaving him wondering how many more there might be. Forcing himself to step toward it, he touched the clear glass cover, letting his fingers glide across the smooth surface. Gripping the handle with his trembling hand, he pulled the door open toward him. The flicker of an interior overhead light confirmed to him that it might be operational.

Though appearing slightly different inside from the others, Sebastian noticed two basic components familiar to him, a pair of headphones and a red-lit keypad. The one clear addition to this chamber was a listing of destinations the others lacked. Included amongst such renowned places as New York, Paris, and Tokyo were Welsh Cove, Maine and Chancellorsville, Nebraska. Remembering his uncle wanting him to return to Nebraska with him, the thought of traveling there through the Daybreak grew in his mind. But he understood this machine wouldn't work for him. Thinking his mom had never been to Nebraska, the certainty of her having no memories to scan of this place left him feeling disappointed. None the less, he climbed in, putting on the headphones in just wanting to pretend for a moment that he could see his dad's childhood home. Pressing the code numbers for Nebraska, Sebastian closed his eyes, anticipating nothing would happen.

Sebastian was startled when feeling a slight jolting pain, like a needle's prick at the back of his head. His eyes opened to bright light blurring his vision. When his sight regained focus, his heart nearly stopped beating when gazing upon the last moments of a brilliant orange twilight. No more than a crest over a field of wind-swept tall grass, the final bursting rays of the setting sun caused him to blink before fading below the distant horizon.

Left amidst the creeping darkness, hearing the serenade of the crickets, in searching around Sebastian found himself standing on a lonely stretch of dirt road. To his right he saw glistening lights straight ahead and the most stars he'd ever seen shimmering above in the night sky. Turning in that direction, he walked along a posted fence until coming to a sign for Chancellorsville, one mile. Urged on by a gusting breeze felt on his back, Sebastian headed toward town, feeling more excited with every step taken.

When reaching his destination, he found Chancellorsville to be no more than a few blocks of buildings and one streetlight, changing from red to green but with no cars passing through the intersection. Window and storefronts all appeared abandoned with the echoing sounds of nearby music rebounding off the walls. Following the melody, he turned down the first corner, smiling in discovering its unexpected origin.

The blinking lights of a Ferris wheel flashed just beyond a moving carousel, the painted horses rising and falling as if in slow motion. Breathing in the wafting aromas of popcorn and other fair delicacies, Sebastian wandered ahead, passing the carnival rides and sideshow tents. But as real as the sights, sounds, and smells seemed, everything in sight appeared dreamlike with no one else in view. Hearing the sounds of joyful screams and laughter over the calls of carnies trying to entice him to play their games became nightmarish. As drawn as he was in finding this place, now escape from here consumed his thoughts. The faster his pace, the louder the voices grew, deafening him when running away at full speed.

Returning to the center of town, Sebastian stopped to catch his breath and try to calm his racing pulse. Sitting down on a bench in front of the general store, he wondered which direction he should go. To the east, the overwhelming darkness caused him a sense of unease. To the west, the horizon still shone a trace of reddish-orange blending in with the dark blue night. Having felt safe in that direction, Sebastian stood up and walked back to where he started out from.

Comforted by the ever-present droning of the crickets and the sounds of his shoes scraping against the dirt road, Sebastian breathed a sigh of relief, although anxious about what lay ahead. Thinking he might have fallen asleep in the Daybreak chamber, he wondered how he could cause himself to wake up before the nightmare would return. Then, seeing the lights from a house just down the road, the desperation to awaken grew.

Halting his steps, after taking a deep breath Sebastian mumbled to himself, "This is just a dream. Nothing in a dream can be harmful. It's just my mind playing tricks on me, my imagination going wild. I just need to calm down."

Hearing what sounded like the slamming of a screen door, Sebastian began walking toward the house lights. Nearing the front yard, he stopped by the mailbox, lit by a porch light. Reading the name, *Dryden*, painted in white on it, he took a few more steps until spying the dancing flames from a fire in the back yard. Intending to walk up to the front door, Sebastian changed his mind once he heard two familiar voices talking.

Treading across the lawn, Sebastian stopped when this scene pixelated before his eyes, fading out for a moment to show him back inside the Daybreak chamber in his dad's lab. The scene then returned as vibrant as before, leading him to believe that he was, in fact, experiencing the Daybreak program and *not* having fallen asleep. He knew how he'd felt before. This proved the same, as real as the other times.

Approaching the back steps of the wrap-around porch, Sebastian's rapidly beating heart nearly exploded in seeing his dad and uncle sitting there. His dad was the first to notice him, slowly rising from his seat, followed by his uncle standing up.

Taking a step back, overcome with rampant thoughts, Sebastian understood what seeing his dad meant. And though knowing what he should say and how he should react, he dismissed both notions when walking up to his dad.

"Hey, kiddo," his dad uttered, clearly stunned to see him. A swift jab of Sebastian's fist to his dad's jaw sent Lee staggering back.

"Damn, I like this kid," Kurt remarked, taking a drink from his beer bottle.

Unsteady on his feet, Lee tried to speak when Sebastian stuck him again, sending his dad down to his knees.

"You're *alive*, and you left me. You let me think you're dead." Sebastian choked out, tears streaming down his face.

Holding out his hand, Lee begged, *"Please, Sebastian,"* before the scene once more pixelated and then vanished before Sebastian's eyes.

Confused by what he'd witnessed, it took Sebastian a few minutes to realize that the Daybreak chamber had turned off. Striking fear into him, he saw how the Daybreak's glass door was shattered and felt the throbbing of his swollen knuckles on his trembling left hand. Forcing the door open, he stumbled out, gripping the side of the chamber with one hand to steady him. Panting to catch his breath, he wiped the tears away from his eyes, closing them until his light-headedness subsided.

***

Wiping the blood from his lip, Lee swallowed hard, understanding none of what had happened. "How the hell did he get here? How did he access the Nebraska program?" Looking to Kurt, he added, "Only you and I and Lydia can enter this program. The only reason Lydia remembers this place is because I brought her here. Sebastian can only enter certain parts of the program because his brainwaves were scanned when Melinda was pregnant with him. But she never came here."

After drinking more of his beer, Kurt revealed, "That's not true."

"What?" Lee quietly uttered.

"That's not true. Melinda did come here, about a month before Sebastian was born. You were in Singapore for a tech convention."

"I don't understand. Why did she come here?"

Kurt answered, "She wanted to try to resolve things between the three of us. Melinda wanted me to come back to San Francisco."

Sighing while rubbing his sore jaw, Lee sat back down, studying his empty beer bottle before tossing it aside. "Well, I guess it all makes sense then. When I scanned Melinda's brainwaves for the Daybreak program a week before she gave birth, her memories of Nebraska were included." Closing his eyes and keeping silent for a minute, Lee then whispered, "Damn."

"What?"

"Kurt, *think* about it. Sebastian just showed up here in the Daybreak program. The *only* machine he could be using is the one in my lab back in San Francisco. Somehow he found his way in."

"*Or* he's with someone who knows how to get in," Kurt reasoned.

Rubbing his forehead as if in pain, Lee responded, "You mean Lexia?"

"Yeah."

Kicking at the burning wood in frustration, Lee mumbled, "I wish Melinda never would have come here. I wish—," his words trailed off.

"Lee, there's something you need to know." Looking at his brother, seeing him nervously shifting his weight from one leg to the other, Lee's jaw dropped when Kurt continued, "Melinda is here. She's been here for a long time."

Chapter Thirteen

"I've been watching you for years. You're an extraordinary hacker who has found his way into *every* program here at Dryden. I would guess that you've hacked into the *Nightfall* program as well."

"Yes," Scotty guardedly confirmed.

"Can you disable it?" Lexia asked, hiding none of the anxiety in her voice.

"No. The program itself is easy to get into once you figure out the password. But deleting or disabling it is designed for only *you* to do, no one else."

"Then tell me the password!"

Sighing, Scotty revealed, "All you have to do is type *your name*."

"*I've done that!*" Lexia angrily yelled.

"I bet you haven't," Scotty calmly responded. "Listen to what I'm saying. You husband had kind of a *strange* sense of humor. And his password is a riddle."

"I don't have time for games!" she interrupted.

"Do you want my help or not?"

"*Yes, of course!*"

"Then calm down and type in these two words, *your* and *name*."

Trying to focus, Lexia took a few deep breaths and did what Scotty told her to. Within an instant of typing the two words *your* and *name*, she gained full access to the *Nightfall* program. Several files instantly flashed on the screen, showing news headlines from around the world and pictures of government officials. As abruptly as they appeared, each image faded, with the screen darkening and the red-lettered word *Nightfall* emerging through the background. But before she could even begin exploring the program, on the opposite side of the desk a two-dimensional holographic image of Lee appeared. "Hello, Lexia. So, you found your way into my lab and database. I'm not surprised. You're one of the smartest people I've ever met."

Just seeing him there before him completely unnerved her. Unable to stop herself, she stretched out her hand. When touching Lee, his virtual image distorted until she pulled her hand away, fearful he might disappear.

"I know why you're here, and I'm not going to stop you. But before you shut *Nightfall* down, there's a few things I need to tell you."

***

Rushing back into the family room, Scotty disrupted a quiet conversation his dads were having. Turning the television back on, he insisted, "We need to keep watching this."

"Why would we want to watch Lexia Dryden's latest arrest?" Xavier asked. "Every time before when she's been arrested, she's always found a way to prove her innocence. This time won't be any different."

"Yes, it will," Scotty corrected him. While fixing his eyes on the television screen, he added, "Sebastian is there with her."

"How do you know?" Abdul questioned.

"I just got off the phone with her?"

"*What!* When did she call you?" Abdul continued.

"Just a few minutes ago. She needed my help in accessing the *Nightfall* program."

Abdul commented, "She can't use a password for that—."

"Unless she was calling from inside Lee's lab," Scotty interrupted, finishing his dad's sentence.

"How could she get in?" Abdul asked. "*Wait.* Never mind, I know how she did it." Looking at both Scotty and Xavier, he explained, "Lee fortified the perimeter walls, floor, and ceiling of his private lab with layers of a unique steel alloy, completely impenetrable. The only way to break in would be to destroy One Legacy Place's self-generating power source, which would disrupt computer programs worldwide, or destroy the tower itself."

"So how did *he* get in?" Xavier asked.

"Advanced security measures he installed center on voice verification and retinal and cornea scans," Abdul answered. "Other than Lee, the only person who could gain access to his lab would be his son. Their voices held similar tones."

"And he has his father's eyes," Xavier added.

Turning the volume low, Scotty and his dads continued watching the dangerous moments escalating outside One Legacy Place. The late molasses-colored afternoon sky, reflecting off the tower, tinted the many windows, causing them to appear as if coated with blood. Threatening the tower's base were armored military support vehicles and tanks with their guns pointed forward. Hovering in the air were attack helicopters sharing flight patterns with government drones. All this and soldiers armed with assault rifles appeared poised for attack

***

Hearing his dad's voice, Sebastian followed the sound until reaching the corner of the super computer. Standing back just enough to stay out of sight, he watched Lexia touch his dad's simulated image. Then fixing his eyes on his dad's face, Sebastian listened to what he needed to say.

"By now, I'm sure you've realized that *Nightfall* was partially created as an act of revenge against you and Lydia. I wanted so much to punish you both for taking my son away from me. From what I later found out, I know you two weren't acting together. Over time I'd hoped that one of you would have slipped up enough to tell me what happened to him, but neither of you did. That was the main reason why I came back to you, the other reason being that I still loved you. Even after all the fights and the separation, I still found myself drawn to you. I can't explain it. Believe me, I've tried to deny it, but I can't. I want to hate you for everything you've done. Why can't I?

After our relationship fell apart the first time, Melinda came along. I stole her from Kurt. Looking back now, I regret that. They were happy together. But for the longest time I had this inflated image of myself, convinced because of my fortune I could have anything I wanted. I was wrong. Melinda and I tried to make a go of it. In the end, though, too many hours spent in the lab or traveling for business drove her away. That, and the ghost of you coming between us, haunted our every moment together. No matter how hard I tried, I still loved you."

Watching Lexia cover her face while bursting into tears, part of him felt sad for her. She had everything she could have wanted, yet somehow found a way to destroy it. But while feeling pity for her, a bigger part of Sebastian was content with how her life lay in ruins.

"The synthetic replicates originally designed through cyber-genetics were never meant for the purposes they eventually served. Our goal had always been to develop the replicates for humanitarian and *strictly* scientific endeavors, keeping humans out of harm's way. Why you allowed corrupt government officials to alter what we sought to create was something I never understood? You already had money and power. What else could they have offered you?

And so this was the other purpose for *Nightfall*, to expose the replicate conspiracy you helped initiate. I hope some justice was served by the world-wide release of classified information. Maybe I was foolish in thinking the world could comprehend the truth. But that's the kind of world I wanted to leave for my daughter and son. Someday people may look back and understand that I wasn't a traitor. I simply wanted to lead a life without lies.

"And speaking of lies, one day, by accident, I found medications you'd hidden behind your nightstand. How many times did I ask you if there was something wrong? You always answered that it was stress. Now I know that you've been diagnosed bipolar. Why didn't you tell me? Why did you keep it a secret? I would have done anything to help you. At least, I would have understood why our relationship suffered as much as it did."

"I wanted to tell you," Sebastian heard Lexia say. "I didn't know how."

"There's something else you should know," Lee continued. "Maybe you've already found out. I wouldn't be surprised if you had. My son, Joshua, is also your biological son. Melinda was never able to conceive a child, so I stole one of your eggs that you had harvested. I never told her. She would never have accepted him if I had. Your egg was implanted in her during what she thought was a fertility treatment. Knowing you never wanted another child, I assumed you wouldn't find out. But now I think you should know, in case there's any chance you'd change your mind and think of trying to find him. He has my eyes and looks a lot like me. And there's a quietness about him which reminds me of you. Even when just four years old, I could see how he wears his heart on his sleeve, which you used to before you built those impenetrable walls to keep your heart from being broken. I miss the person who hides behind them."

Stunned by the revelation that Lexia was his biological mother, Sebastian's legs nearly gave out. Breathing hard while staggering back, he managed to walk over to the elevator doors, resting his head against them. Confused on how to feel about this, he wanted to get away, not knowing how Lexia would react. And with his anger toward his dad growing, having been lied to about the woman he thought was his mother, Sebastian wondered if his dad would ever have told him the truth. Why was he so willing to condemn Lexia for lying, while he was so willing to keep lies of his own? When did keeping secrets from someone, ever truly protect them?

***

"So now we come to the point where we say goodbye," Lee said, smiling. "Press the enter key when you're ready."

Feeling panicked by his words, Lexia's mind reeled with thoughts of what would come next. Her sole purpose for the last several months had been the need to silence the *Nightfall* data breach once and for all. Yet now the reality that she'd never see Lee again, as well as all he'd revealed, complicated her desire to destroy the last thing keeping him alive in her mind. She knew that Lee and Lydia were already gone and the only part of her life left was the boy she tried to kill, her son.

Consumed with guilt in understanding the only way Sebastian could ever stay alive would be with the disabling and termination of *Nightfall*, Lexia initiated the final sequence. After pressing the enter key, Lee instructed, "All you need to do to stop *Nightfall* is by voice recognition in saying the word 'please.' A deactivation confirmation message will instantly be sent to the Secretary General of the United Nations and the President of the United States. Say the magic word and everything goes away. Say it. That's why you're here."

Swallowing deep, Lexia's first attempt to say it wasn't even audible. Trying again, this time she uttered loud enough to hear, "Please."

"Goodbye, Lexia. I love you," Lee said with his holographic image vanishing. Behind her, all the lights on the super computer blinked in unison before going dark. There in front of her, Lee's laptop turned off, leaving her to see her faint reflection on the black screen.

Gripped by overwhelming sadness and anger, Lexia agonizingly screamed out. Reaching for Lee's laptop computer, she hurled it through the air. Colliding against the wall of video monitors, an explosion of sparks showered to the floor when it smashed the glass of two monitors. Slamming her fists hard against the frosted glass top of his desk, it shattered, jagged edges, slicing her hands. Holding them in front of her face, her eyes firmly watched blood seeping down across her palms.

As her rage intensified, all rational thought seemed to disappear. Feeling as though living through a nightmare, Lexia pushed over what remained of the desk, sending shards of glass spraying across the floor. Then picking up the chair, she threw it with all her strength, sending it soaring through the air until striking another work station. Expelling an ear-splitting shriek from her lungs, she teetered with lightheadedness and fell back against the super computer.

Spent of her energy, Lexia dropped to her knees, growing disoriented with her surroundings. Shifting her eyes and turning her face in both directions, the rapidly spinning room began refocusing in her eyes with clarity soon returning to her rampant thoughts. And luring her further away from her episode of dementia, was the sound of the elevator doors opening. Stumbling to stand, when finally staggering near them, her heart sank, seeing Sebastian's frightened stare as the elevator doors closed with him inside.

Chapter Fourteen

Hearing Lexia pounding on the other side of the elevator doors, Sebastian shuddered in fear, barely understanding the voice requesting, "Destination, please."

Blankly, he answered, "As far away as possible."

"Please select from the provided directory."

Searching around, he spotted the floor directory just off to the side of the elevator doors. Trailing his finger down the listing, considering where he might be able to escape, he rejected selecting both the underground parking decks and the main lobby. "How do I get away from here?" he mumbled in frustration under his breath. Closing his eyes, Sebastian thought for a minute, reasoning he had no idea how to escape from here alone. Wondering of how surrounded they most likely were by replicates, he admitted, "I can't do this without her."

Finding the courage to request the opening of the elevator doors, the overhead light dimmed, flickering as if running out of power. "Open doors," Sebastian commanded, yet they remained closed. Trying to pry them open, an electric charge singed his fingertips, forcing him to pull back his hands.

Shifting his eyes around, Sebastian hoped there might be a rooftop door hidden by the elevator ceiling tiles. Jumping up, he dislodged one of the tiles enough to see red light faintly shining down through. Searching for anything he could use to climb, he decided to use his belt, unfastening and dragging it from around his waist. Making a loop and tossing it up, it fell back to him. But when tossing it a second time, the loop hooked on to something he couldn't see. Tugging on his belt, not knowing if it would hold his weight, Sebastian took the chance and climbed hand-over-fist. Grabbing at the first thing he felt, his belt let loose while straining for a better grip. Grimacing, he pulled himself further up, breaking through the ceiling tiles and then crawling out the top of the elevator.

Glancing above into the elevator shaft, four large cables seemed to disappear into the darkness a few flights overhead. Turning toward a small red light positioned just out of reach, he noticed the metal rungs of a maintenance ladder, bolted into the concrete. Grasping the rung nearest him, Sebastian took a deep breath before beginning to scale the ladder, knowing it led up, but not knowing what he would find there in the dark.

***

While intensely staring at the television screen, the live footage from One Legacy Place blurred and pixelated before fading from view. "*What just happened?*" Scotty burst out. Frantically checking the cable connections, nothing appeared unusual. Then finding his cell phone, he tried pulling up the footage on social media, but connecting to the internet failed. "*I don't understand this!*"

With Xavier having discovered a similar issue with his cell phone, Abdul, while not able to access the live footage, at least still had service. "I'm going to call Maurice," Abdul said, hoping this would calm Scotty. "Maurice, this is Abdul Nassir. I require your assistance."

"Of course, Mister Nassir, how may I be of service?"

"I have lost access to live news footage of the crisis at One Legacy Place in San Francisco."

"You and the entire world, sir. All major networks, as well as a majority of social media outlets, are linked to Dryden Technologies programming and software. The internal self-generating fusion power source at One Legacy Place has been disabled, resulting in a catastrophic worldwide technology crisis, most significant in Asia, North America, and Europe."

"How are governments dealing with this crisis?" Abdul asked.

"Existing emergency protocols for such disturbances are currently being enacted. I am informed that both Hong Kong and Tokyo will be back on line within the hour. It may take up to twenty-four hours for the rest of the world to follow."

"Are you able to tell how the power source at One Legacy Place was disabled?"

"Of course, sir. It was done so by military assault."

***

Breathing hard, Sebastian pressed on, climbing rung after rung in the pitch blackness of the elevator shaft. Wondering how long he'd been climbing, he looked down, thinking he'd see the red light from where he started out. But the light was gone, leaving him feeling disoriented and scared.

When reaching up for the next rung, Sebastian nearly lost grip by a tremoring sensation shaking the walls. He could hear sounds of distant thunder and felt dirt and dust falling onto him. The heavy air he breathed in was soon tainted by the faint stench of smoke. Fearing there might be a fire somewhere close, he continued on, trying to quicken his pace.

When he had climbed to the next level, Sebastian felt the cold steel of the elevator doors. Each attempt to open them failed, some scorching his fingers with electrical charges and others simply not parting even an inch. As he continued climbing, the elevator shaft became more like a tomb, with his thoughts being drawn to the idea that this could be his final resting place. Maybe this is what it's like when you first die, all consuming blackness.

The effects of his Parkinson's disease grew more severe. The tremors causing Sebastian's hands to shake made gripping the metal ladder rungs difficult. The light-headedness he experienced matched his loss of energy. Feeling lethargic with his movements, Sebastian stopped climbing, holding on with what strength he had left. "I can't do this anymore," he whispered, almost out of breath.

While remaining still, Sebastian noticed how the air was growing warmer, with the faint stench of smoke smelling more pungent. Glancing up, thinking he might see the flickering light from a fire, all he saw was the same darkness surrounding him. Disheartened by not having found a way out of the elevator shaft, he wondered if it was worth climbing further. What if when reaching the top, he couldn't find a way out? Then what? With these doubts troubling him, the notion of climbing down and returning to the elevator crossed him mind. But then he heard sounds echoing from below.

Panicked, he first worried that the replicate soldiers had found their way inside. One thing Sebastian knew for certain of was that if captured, he'd most likely be killed. Guessing the tower had been evacuated when the fire alarms sounded out, anyone left inside would be a potential witness. It seemed unlikely the replicates would allow that.

Listening to the sounds coming from below, Sebastian tried judging how close the replicate had gained on him. Swallowing hard, he reached up, feeling for the next rung. Wrapping his fingers around it, it felt warm to the touch in a way the other rungs hadn't felt. If there was indeed a fire, then he was getting closer to it.

Sudden blasts from a barrage of gunfire and the piercing sounds of bullets ricocheting deafened Sebastian, leaving him wincing from the painful ringing in his ears. Fearfully glancing down, sparks lit the darkness below from the violent firing exchange. But maybe it wasn't meant to be an exchange? Possibly replicates were mistakenly shooting at each other and hopefully would suffer enough damage to disable them. While this seemed unlikely, nothing there in the pitch black was certain.

Grabbing the next rung, Sebastian forced himself to climb higher. Arriving at another elevator exit, he cautiously touched the metal door, crying out in pain from touching the blistering surface. With his chest heaving and his head throbbing, Sebastian reached up again as the gun battle below sporadically continued. Anxiously wanting to put some distance between him and the replicates, he continued climbing for what seemed like an eternity.

Sebastian lost count of the number of elevator doors he'd passed and failed to open. While noticing how hot the air was to breathe in, when risking touching another elevator exit doors, the metal felt cooler. Prying at the doors, at first they wouldn't part. But when trying again, a sliver of light shone into the dark shaft. Forcing them further open, Sebastian parted them just enough to squeeze his body through. And when crawling out, the jaw-dropping view robbed him of his breath and strength.

***

"Sir, there is something else of interest that you had previously requested I monitor."

"That being?"

"*Nightfall* has been disabled. Both the White House and the United Nations have received confirmation." After a pause, Maurice continued, "I must also now amend information proven false from seemingly reliable sources."

"Meaning *what*?" Abdul questioned.

"*Credible* sources, both congressional and from the President's cabinet are at this moment refuting published reports regarding General Jaclyn Reddinger exoneration with charges stemming from her involvement with the replicate crisis. She continues to be found guilty of all charges and warrants have been issued for her immediate arrest. Shoot-to-kill orders have also been given should she fail to surrender."

"But with military support, forces under her command have attacked One Legacy Place," Abdul uttered with disbelief.

"That is incorrect, sir. It is now being reported that the assault on One Legacy Place has been carried out by a replicate para-military force. The government is currently scrambling jet fighters to engage the replicates. Also, ground assault troops as closing in on downtown San Francisco as we speak."

Chapter Fifteen

The glass from each of the floor to ceiling windows on the upper observation floor had been blasted away, coating the marble floor tiles with sharp, glistening shards. Charred remnants of the white and black décor were strewn about, ruined beyond recognition. Fractured plaster fell in pieces from the ceiling, with a large beam appearing ready to collapse without warning. Rising from a gaping hole were flames and smoked from a fire burning on the lower level.

Yet it was not seeing this destruction that caused Sebastian to stand paralyzed with fear. Noticing it hovering there in the darkness outside, he'd fallen under the stare of the pilot, waiting for his body to be riddled with bullets from the high-powered guns attached to the attack helicopter. Flinching when sparks exploded from exposed electrical wires, Sebastian's breath rushed from his body, his heart sinking in his chest as this moment agonizingly dragged on. "He won't pull the trigger until I tell him to," he jumped, hearing a woman's voice call out.

Seeing a black woman, dressed in a black military uniform, stepping out from the shadows near a fire escape stairwell, Sebastian held still. While pointing a pistol at him, she ordered, "Slowly walk toward me. Don't take your eyes off me or I'll shoot."

Hearing broken glass crushing under his shoes, as Sebastian stepped toward her he whispered, *"Please—."*

"I didn't tell you to talk," she calmly interrupted him.

Feeling his head spinning, Sebastian stopped walking as he tried to maintain his balance. "I just want to go home," he mumbled.

"Shut up or I'll shoot you!" she bellowed.

Quaking uncontrollably, as he approached her, she ordered, "Stop. Turn around." With his back to her, Sebastian thought he heard her stepping closer. "Now, we wait," she added. "I'm told she'll be here any time. If you even *think* of telling her that I'm standing behind you then you'll be dead before you hit the ground."

Glancing down to the lower level, Sebastian's eyes fixed on the flames burning something unrecognizable and plumes of smoke rising and clouding his forward view. Both reminded him of the campfire his dad started the night before being invited to the Lesterman farm. Like so many other times, he wondered how things would have been if they'd chosen not to do certain things or go to the places they went. Sebastian remembered hearing someone once say that hindsight was twenty-twenty. One could look back and see exactly what they should have done. But thinking of all that had happened to him, understanding what he should have done different held no clarity, other than never having been born.

"Who are you?" the woman asked, startling him from his thoughts.

"I'm no one special."

"What's your name?"

"Sebastian."

"I see your hands are shaking. Are you scared?"

"Yes."

"Are you afraid to die?"

Thinking for a moment, Sebastian responded, "No."

"Why not?"

"Because living is scarier."

"I don't think you'll have to worry about that much longer."

Pausing, he then uttered, "Thank you."

"For what?"

"Putting an end to this."

"*Interesting!*" she remarked. "I've actually never met someone who wanted to die."

Calmly, Sebastian responded, "I'm already dead."

"Then you won't feel a thing."

Hearing sounds from below, Sebastian and the woman silenced their conversation. Then to his left, Sebastian spied Lexia slowly climbing what was left of a circular staircase. But instead of approaching him, she wandered over to the opposite side of the gaping hole in the floor he stood in front of. He instantly noticed red blood staining the left shoulder of her white blouse.

From behind her back, Lexia revealed a small black gun, keeping it pointed down to the floor. Looking at her, her face appeared expressionless, her eyes vacant. "How did you get out of the lab?" Sebastian finally asked.

"After the power went out, I was able to pry the elevator doors open," she flatly answered. "I got out the same way you did. A few replicates found their way into the elevator shaft—but I took care of them," she said, motioning with her gun in suggesting how.

"So now what?" Sebastian asked.

"Now all this comes to an end." Then raising her gun, Lexia pointed it at him. "I'm sorry, Sebastian, for everything."

Saying nothing, Sebastian closed his eyes and waited. A click sounding out reminded him of the woman pointing a gun at his back, leaving him to guess which one of them would shoot him first. Hearing a gunshot, he flinched to his right, feeling the bullet pass by his ear. The next sounds heard were ones of gasping. Turning around, Sebastian saw that Lexia's bullet had struck the woman behind him, tearing through her throat. Having fallen to her knees, holding her blood-soaked hands to her neck, her body slumped to the floor, convulsing and then becoming still.

Looking back to Lexia, Sebastian uttered, "How did you know she was behind me?"

Showing no emotion, Lexia replied, "I didn't know she was standing behind you. I wanted to end your suffering. I was aiming for you."

Before he could respond to her answer, what appeared to be a streak of lightning struck the back of the attack helicopter, sending it into a tail spin. With no time to react, Sebastian fell back as the helicopter crashed into the floor below theirs. The jarring impact sent the overhead beam down, knocking Lexia off the upper floor. Several floors under the helicopter wreckage gave way, collapsing under them, causing the tower to sway.

Sitting up, covered and cut by glass, Sebastian saw Lexia clinging for her life to the fallen beam. Seeing the emergency stairwell door swinging open, Sebastian's first thought was to run toward it. But catching the desperation in Lexia's eyes made him stay. Ducking away from showering sparks, he edged closer to the beam, keeping his eyes of her as she struggled to hold on. Trying to reach his hand out, the distance between them proved too far apart. Standing up, Sebastian maneuvered around some debris, attempting to get closer to her. Again, reaching out his hand, the space between them seemed much shorter, but Lexia was still out of reach.

Scooting on his knees to a jagged spot he thought would be the closest to her, Sebastian strained to reach out his hand one more time. This time, the tips of her fingers brushed against the tips of his. But when watching her eyes, the desperation they exuded altered to hopelessness with her grip on the beam failing.

Understanding her sad expression, he calmly said, "I forgive you. It's okay, Mom, you can let go."

Clearly startled by what he said, Lexia's fingers slipped from their hold as she fell toward the burning helicopter wreckage several floors down. Sebastian quickly turned away, hearing nothing other than the roar of the flames and the distant echoes of sirens.

***

Gazing out over the placid water to the evergreens lining the nearest shore, Scotty watched as a veil of fog steamed up from the ocean, clouding the trees just enough to make them appear as if faint ghosts. The stillness of the air was broken by the flight of an eagle, the flapping of its wings sounding out until gliding over the water's surface. Its talons disturbed the water, capturing a fish and then flying off.

Glancing down at the wet stones under his shoes, Scotty leaned forward, seeing his reflection's fluid motion in the grey sound, drawing its color from the sky. His lifeless expression mirror how he felt inside since seeing the devastating damage the replicate soldiers inflicted upon the once impressive One Legacy Place. In truth, it wasn't the building he mourned, but the friend lost to him. Although Sebastian's body had not been recovered from the ruins, both Scotty and his dads believed he hadn't survived. At Abdul's request, Maurice had conducted an extensive search of San Francisco's surveillance video archive spanning several hours after human military forces had defeated the replicate army securing the tower. Not one camera anywhere in the city had captured Sebastian's image after the battle. Several cameras did, in fact, show him entering One Legacy Place with Lexia, confirming her claim he was there with her. As for Lexia, herself, her charred remains had been located several floors below the upper observation floor.

Studying the cover of a book Sebastian had given him, Scotty silently read the title, *Brave New World*, before tossing the book into the water. Knowing his world without Sebastian would never be the same, he couldn't bear to open the cover. He didn't want to know what a new world might be like. He wanted the old one back.

He thought the book would sink, but it resisted and began floating out in the subtle current. Watching it drift away, Scotty imagined its pages as messages sent without a bottle, wondering if it would someday be found, washing ashore to someone in a far land. Would the ink wash clean of the pages? Would the next reader only be able to read the words printed on the cover, leaving them to ponder what kind of new world the book could no longer reveal? Maybe it was best that way, not spoiling their world with troubling thoughts and ideas.

Swallowing hard, Scotty's jaw quivered as he whispered, "Goodbye, Sebastian." He wanted to say more, but his throat constricted further words from finding their voice.

Chapter Sixteen

May, seven months later

After making his way through the forest, Sebastian found the clearing where he and his dad had camped months ago. Closing his eyes, he tried recalling the sounds and smell of the wood burning and the memory of his dad tucking him into his sleeping bag. Tall grass and colorful spring flowers swayed in the gentle breeze, being shadowed for a moment as a large white fair-weather cloud blocked the sun and then drifted away. Wandering around, Sebastian soon discovered a circle of stones his dad once set to contain their campfire. Picking up one of the smaller ones, he studied its smooth surface before stuffing it in his pocket. Taking one last glance around, Sebastian then turned away, knowing he'd never see this place again.

Passing through more trees and brush, he soon came to the road and headed north. Never thinking he could find the courage to return to the Lesterman farm, this intended destination took only a few minutes walking time to arrive at. Having learned that Ben Lesterman had escaped from one of Dryden's replicate facilities, Sebastian wondered if he'd found his way home. He, himself, tried going home before, but was unable to resume the life he once led. Would it be different for Ben?

Approaching the mailbox at the end of the driveway, Sebastian halted his stride when seeing a German shepherd scamper up to him, playfully nudging his hand. Stroking its soft coat ushered happy memories back to Sebastian. The dog reminded him of Silas, but had more dark brown fur around his eyes.

"Sage!" a man's voice hollered. At first the dog ignored the man's call, but then returned to his owner, though looking back at Sebastian.

With his eyes fixed on the dog, Sebastian didn't notice when its owner stepped into view. "Hello!" he called out.

Glancing over to a familiar old pickup truck, Sebastian watched Ben Lesterman wipe the grime off his hands from fixing something under the hood. Smiling as he approached, Ben commented, "Sage must really like you. I've never seen him *not* bark at someone."

"You have a nice dog," Sebastian mumbled, averting his eyes.

Noticing his tremoring hands, Ben assured him, "You don't have to be scared of me. I'm not going to hurt you. Are you lost?"

"No, I'm just passing through."

"You seem kind of young to be out here alone."

Sebastian shrugged his shoulders without saying anything. Feeling the dog nudge his hand again, he ran his fingers through the fur on its head, causing it to wag its tail, enjoying the attention.

"You've definitely made a friend. I just got Sage from a guy about a mile away. A few years back I got his brother from the same litter, but he's gone. I don't know what happened to him." Attempting to break the awkward silence, Ben then asked, "Do you want something to eat? I have a pot of beef stew simmering on the stove."

Seeing the house in the background and remembering all that happened inside, Sebastian lost his nerve to be here. His curiosity had been satisfied, seeing that Ben had in fact come home and at least, on the surface, seemed to be living the life he once may have had here. His childhood memories of this place must have been strong enough for him to overcome what he found when he returned.

"No thank you. I should be going," Sebastian quietly responded.

"Where are you heading? Could I at least drive you somewhere?"

Unsure of what to say, Sebastian shook his head and began walking away. Feeling a hand grip his shoulder, he turned around, seeing a concerned expression on Ben's face. "Take care, kid. It's not safe out there," he warned.

"I know. I'll be okay."

Sighing, Ben commented, "Damn, you've been through a lot. I can see it in your eyes. What's your name, kid?"

"Sebastian."

"Come on inside."

Taking a step back, Sebastian shook his head.

"I'm sorry," Ben apologized. "It's okay. I understand." Rubbing the back of his neck with his hand, Ben then extended the other hand to Sebastian. "At least we could part as friends." Guardedly, Sebastian shook his hand, causing Ben to smile. "Take care. If you need anything, come back. My door will always be open to survivors like us."

"Thanks."

Looking down at his dog, Ben urged, "Come on Sage," waving goodbye to Sebastian while walking back to his pickup truck.

***

August

Setting her book down next to her on the sofa, Melinda stretched and stood up. Walking across the living room, she turned her head to look out the front window and nearly fainted when seeing Sebastian standing out by the mailbox. After finding out he'd died at One Legacy Place, she thought she, herself, had died with him, again mourning the loss of her child. But there he stood, impossibly alive. Or maybe he was a ghost meant to haunt her. She deserved as much.

Cautiously creeping over to the front door, from behind the yellow curtains, she spied out at her son. Dressed in light-blue jeans and a grey cut-off t-shirt over his lean frame, his longish hair from under the baseball cap worn backwards on his head and the shadow of a beard on his face made him appear like a handsome young version of Lee. With his hand resting on the white picket gate, he seemed afraid to open it.

Wanting more than anything to step out onto the porch to greet him, Melinda froze when touching the doorknob. Fearful of frightening him away, she had no idea what to say to him. *How will he react when seeing me?* She wondered. *How do I tell him I'm sorry for everything that happened to him? And...would he stay if I asked him to, no, begged him to?*

For years she'd carried guilt about the night she thought he died in the car accident. Had she not plotted to steal away with him and Kurt, he would have been safe. Kurt later told her, however, of Lydia's plan to have Joshua kidnapped, reasoning with her how everything was beyond their control. Yet knowing that didn't help rid her of the shame she felt.

From behind, Kurt startled her when wrapping her in his arms. "I'm sorry," he apologized with a grin. "I didn't mean to scare you. What are you looking at?"

"Sebastian," she choked out.

"Oh, my God," Kurt breathlessly uttered. "I can't believe it."

Bursting into tears, Melinda panicked, *"I can't go outside! I can't talk to him! I don't know what to say! How could he ever forgive me?"*

"Stay here. Let me talk to him," Kurt urged, trying to calm her. Backing away, Melinda held her breath, watching as Kurt opened the door.

***

Sebastian saw Kurt step outside, his uncle clearly surprised. "Sebastian, wow, I don't know what to say. How? I found out from Scotty that you had died at the assault on One Legacy Place. It destroyed him. How did you survive? My god, where have you been?"

I'm not sure I did survive, Sebastian thought to himself. He ignored his uncle's questions and instead quietly said, "I guess this place is real."

"It is," Kurt responded with a smile and anxiously added, "Do want to come in?"

Shaking his head, Sebastian answered, "No."

Stepping closer, Kurt placed his hand next to Sebastian's on the gate. "Please come inside. This could be your home, if you want it to be."

Glancing slightly away, Sebastian responded, "No, I don't belong here."

"Yes, you do. Come inside. We can talk about it."

Answering without words, Sebastian took a step back. He then asked a question burning his lips. "Is my dad here?"

"No."

"When did you last see him?"

Exhaling deep, Kurt answered while looking away, "It's been a while."

"Do you know where he's at?"

"Yeah. Do you want to see him?"

"No."

"Sebastian, please come inside," Kurt begged. "There's so much you need to know. There's so much I need to tell you. I can help you understand all this."

Stepping back again, Sebastian shook his head.

"I'm sorry," his uncle offered. "I'm not trying to scare you. I just want you to stay…but I guess that's not gonna happen."

Swallowing hard, Sebastian wasn't sure what to say next until his uncle asked, "If I see your dad again, do you have anything you want me to say to him?"

Thinking this over, Sebastian answered, "Tell him I'm sorry for punching him."

"Don't be. He deserved it."

Sebastian sort of grinned at hearing this. Stepping further away, he stopped for a moment when hearing his uncle claim, "Your mom is inside."

Not believing him while thinking of Lexia, Sebastian continued walking, mumbling under his breath, "No she's not."

***

After walking out of the barn, Kurt could tell his brother was surprised to see him.

"It's been awhile," Lee commented.

"A few months."

"Seems like just yesterday," Lee responded with sarcasm. "How's Melinda?"

"She's had a rough day."

"Why?"

Having not revealed to Lee all that happened at One Legacy Place, Lee continued withholding what he knew and answered, "Sebastian showed up at the farm today."

Seeming robbed of his breath, Lee struggled in asking, "How is he?"

"That kid's been through hell," Kurt responded. "I've never seen someone so lost."

"What about his Parkinson's?"

"I didn't ask him about it, but his hands were trembling and he looked real tired. I don't think it's gotten any worse since I saw him last—but I don't know for sure."

"D-did he say anything about me?" Lee could hardly ask, barely controlling his emotions.

"He wanted me to tell you that he was sorry for punching you."

Releasing a nervous laugh, Lee responded, "I deserved it."

"That's what I told him."

"So, Melinda saw him. What did she say to him?"

Sighing, Kurt answered, "She only saw him through the window. She was too scared to talk to him, and he wouldn't come in." Continuing, Kurt revealed, "I told him she was there, but I don't think he believed me. He just left, mumbling something under his breath I couldn't hear."

"*What do you mean he left?*" Lee angrily asked. "Why didn't you make him stay?"

"He wouldn't," Kurt calmly responded. "Nothing I could have said would have made him stay. I wanted to tell him about you and Lydia but I didn't. I'll keep your secret. And speaking of secrets, *Nightfall* has been disabled."

"I knew it would be. I just regret that Lexia forced Sebastian to help her do it."

"Lexia is dead."

At first appearing stunned, Lee sighed and responded, "Good," and then asked, "How did she die?"

Bending the truth, Kurt answered, "An assassin killed here."

"Please tell me Sebastian wasn't with her when it happened."

This time Kurt lied. "No, he wasn't."

"I hope she enjoyed the last words I left for her."

"What did you say?"

"I told her that even though I hated her, I also still loved her. I'm sure she probably didn't believe it, but I wanted to make her pay one last time for everything she put me through."

"And what if she *did* believe it?"

Lee shrugged his shoulders as he looked away.

After silent moments passed, still feeling the tension between them, Kurt changed the subject. "As you requested, both your and Lydia's bodies have been moved to Montreal. When I last talked to Sidney, he-or she rather, confirmed both your life supports systems were working fine. There's been no change with your conditions. Lydia shows no signs of recovering from her severe head trauma and as for you, both your heart and lungs will never be able to be disconnected from life support. I guess the only lives you and Lydia will ever be able to lead will be here in the Daybreak chamber." Curiously looking around, Kurt asked, "Where *is* Lydia?"

"We're playing hide-n-seek," Lee answered. "She's a lot better at this than I thought."

***

Stepping out of the barn, Kurt stopped for a moment, holding onto the wooden door. Shaking his head, he turned around, walking back inside. Approaching his Daybreak chamber, he stared at it for the longest time, tapping his fingers on the glass door. Then reaching behind it, he found the electrical outlet, hesitating for a moment but then pulling the plug on the machine. "I'm sorry, Lee," he whispered. "I can't do this anymore. I'm done."

***

Blinking her eyes open, Lydia saw a smiling face watching her. "Hi, Aunt Sidney," she groggily said, rubbing the sleepiness from her eyes.

"Hello, gorgeous! How are you feeling, sweetheart?"

"I'm tired."

"Of course you are, you poor dear."

Leaning her head to the side, Lydia saw her dad lying next to her. "Is Daddy still sleeping?"

Now forcing a smile, Sidney answered, "He's very tired, precious." Trying to change the subject, Sidney showed something to her. "I bet you remember this." Holding Lydia's rag doll out to her, Sidney said, "Your brother left this for you."

"Alice!" Lydia exclaimed. Then looking around, she asked, "Where is Sebastian?"

"He went away for a while, but he wanted to make sure you had your doll before he left."

"When will he come back?"

Unnerved by this question, Sidney forced a smile and responded, "I don't know, sweetheart. *Oh, well*, I guess you're just stuck with me."

"You need a make-over," Lydia giggled, looking at Sidney's head full of curlers.

"Honey, ain't that the truth."

***

December

Having arrived just after nightfall, Sebastian spent hours sitting on the docks and wandering the quiet streets of Sea Bridge, passing by darkened shopfront windows and a number of houses decorated for the holiday. In truth, not until entering a church at midnight did he realize it was Christmas. Finding a seat in a secluded part of the sanctuary, he quietly sat, listening to songs of rejoice sung in harmony by the choir and hearing the words of the priest, his message of peace and good will to his gathered midnight mass congregation.

For well over a year, he had wandered the country, finding answers to a few questions, but mostly drifting from town to town. Never staying in one place for more a week, if that, working odd jobs helped earn money for food. Yet when haunted by restless thoughts and things reminding him of those he had loved and lost, Sebastian again and again tried escaping. After a certain point, though, in knowing his ghosts would never leave, he decided it was time to return to Alaska. Maybe he could try again to make this place home.

It wasn't until a quarter past three in the morning when he snuck in Scotty's house, using the spare key under the welcome mat. Stepping into the living room, he saw the low flames in the fireplace, burning what remained of a large log. As welcoming as the fire felt from being out in the cold, capturing his attention was the Christmas tree set in the corner. Light from multi-colored bulbs glistened off shiny ornaments and shimmering strands of tinsel. Not having had a Christmas tree before, he imagined he'd remember this moment for the rest of his life.

But something he never imagined happening occurred when hearing a sound behind him. Limping into view was the one present he most wanted. Reaching out his hand, Silas licked his finger and then nudged him, wanting to be petted. Sitting down, with his back resting against the sofa, Silas laid his head in Sebastian's lap, both happy to receive the love they both desperately missed.

"I met your brother," Sebastian whispered to his dog. "I'm not gonna leave you again," he added, seeing Silas's gentle eyes watching him. "I promise."

***

Hearing sounds from downstairs, always a light sleeper, Xavier rolled over, looking at their digital clock. "Dear God, it's the dead of night," he sleepily mumbled. Poking at Abdul, he growled, "Go tell your son to go back to bed. Christmas doesn't start until eight and not until after I've had my coffee."

Sighing, Abdul yawningly answered, "Yes dear," as he stumbled out of bed.

Half-asleep while walking downstairs, when stepping into the living room, he fully awakened, stunned by hearing Sebastian quietly talking to Silas. Moving around the corner of the sofa, Sebastian looked up at him before standing. Seeing Sebastian's eyes glassy and wet, Abdul listened as he softly whispered, "Is it alright if I come home?"

Pulling Sebastian to him, feeling his body trembling, Abdul, barely controlling his emotions, answered, "You're *my* son now. This will *always* be your home. *Forever.*"

"Okay," Sebastian faintly mumbled.

Easing down with him on the sofa, Abdul held him close while tugging at a quilt to cover them. "I know your father told you that he would protect you and that nothing would happen. I know how much he loved you and how hard he tried to keep you safe. All I can promise is to try to do the same. With all the strength I possess, I vow to do all I can to protect you."

"What if you can't?"

"I refuse to even think about that. I won't let anything harm you. You have my word." Holding Sebastian's quaking hand and seeing how tired his eyes looked, Abdul insisted, "Come on. You can sleep in the guest bedroom."

"Will you stay with me until I fall asleep?"

Smiling, Abdul responded, "All night. I'll be there in the morning when you wake up. I'm not going anywhere."

Seeming more exhausted, Sebastian mumbled, "Thank you."

The End

About Jeffery Martin Botzenhart

Well, here we are again at the end of another book. I know where this is going, *you* asking a bunch of questions about me…and *me* spilling my innermost secrets. If you've read my other books, by now you know there isn't much to tell. I'm married, have three sons, am college educated, and live in Ohio. Oh, but I know you. You wish to probe into the mind of the genius who wrote the masterpiece you just finished reading…or something to that effect. So let's cross the line and delve deeper. My favorite color is turquoise, favorite food is spaghetti, favorite dessert is anything with Oreos, and favorite movie is *The Princess Bride*. Now it's your turn. What? *Nothing*? I pour my heart out to you and I get *nothing*? I guess I understand. I'll be okay. But should you change your mind, remember that talking to a book in public may not be socially acceptable. I don't judge…but others might.

Social Media Links

Facebook:
https://www.facebook.com/jefferymartinbotzenhartwritingjourney/

If you enjoyed this story, check out these other Solstice Publishing books by Jeffery Martin Botzenhart:

Daybreak – Nightfall Book One

Amidst a world of cyber surveillance and advancing technology of 2035 San Francisco, Sebastian, a teen runaway, innocently access a sophisticated virtual reality program. The breach of this data proves the catalyst in unraveling corporate and government sanctioned deception of the most unimaginable type. And along with his computer hacker friend, Scotty, both are thrust into a dangerous conspiracy, linking them to a source exposing the truth.

https://bookgoodies.com/a/B073SB9BXG

After Dark – Nightfall Book Two

With Sebastian's health deteriorating, his dad decides to risk them both crossing into Canada in efforts to meet with a physician friend in Montreal who might be able to help. Yet before even reaching the border they encounter new threats against them. Their escape is further complicated when after reaching Lee's friend they are separated. This leads Sebastian to a perilous journey across the Canadian frontier, finding both a new friend and discovering a far more dangerous robotic conspiracy than anyone could have imagined.

https://bookgoodies.com/a/B0778SL11P

Harvest Fever

A bullied and abused teen boy's plans for escape from a small remote town in Appalachia are hindered by a space alien invasion. Finding everyone in town missing, the aliens begin hunting him. And after being captured, he discovers the unimaginable truth of what's really going on.

https://bookgoodies.com/a//B074JZV44F